PASSPORT TO FEAR

Rose and Ray, two young women travelling by ship from India to England are alike in appearance. Both orphans, Ray is wealthy, while Rose has lived on her wits. Ray has a heart condition and is going to England to her guardian. But then when she dies Rose takes on the other girl's identity. However, in England Rose becomes a victim of her new guardian's greed and her life is threatened. Can she yet find love and happiness?

PATRICIA HUTCHISON

PASSPORT TO FEAR

Complete and Unabridged

LINFORD
Leicester

First published in Great Britain in 1974 by
Robert Hale Limited
London

First Linford Edition
published 2008
by arrangement with
Robert Hale Limited
London

British Library CIP Data

Hutchison, Patricia
    Passport to fear.—Large print ed.—
Linford romance library
    1. Identity theft—Fiction 2. Guardian and
ward—Fiction 3. Romantic suspense novels
4. Large type books
I. Title
823.9'14 [F]

ISBN 978–1–84782–296–3

Published by
F. A. Thorpe (Publishing)
Anstey, Leicestershire

Set by Words & Graphics Ltd.
Anstey, Leicestershire
Printed and bound in Great Britain by
T. J. International Ltd., Padstow, Cornwall

This book is printed on acid-free paper

1

Rose Delmont sat on the side of her bunk in the comfortable two-berthed cabin, and looked enviously at the girl opposite. The ship was two days out from Bombay on its way to England, and both girls had suffered rather badly from sea-sickness. But now, the worst over, they were just beginning to take an interest in their surroundings and each other.

The stewardess had jollied them both into getting up and dressing; telling them at the same time that once they were up on deck the fresh breezes would put new life into them.

Rose looked again at her cabin companion who was now languidly sliding into some of the loveliest and most expensive 'undies' Rose had ever seen. She glanced down furtively at her own skimpy nylon slip, then stood up shakily and pulled a pink linen frock over her head. At least the top layer is all right, she thought weakly, sitting down again and looking about her for her suitcase.

'They've put the baggage under the wrong berths,' remarked the other girl, whose name as yet Rose did not know. 'See, here is your case if that is what you are looking for.' She had what Rose would have called a real 'pukka-sahib' voice. 'What's your name?'

Rose told her, vaguely resenting her companion's superior manner. The girl stared at Rose for a moment in silence, then gave a short laugh.

'Anything funny about it?' Rose asked sharply, her irritation gaining the upper hand for the moment.

'No, no, of course not,' replied the other hastily. 'It's just that — well, my name is Ray Desmond. The two names, yours and mine, are rather alike, I thought. Rose Delmont, Ray Desmond. D'you see what I mean?'

Rose nodded indifferently. About the

only thing that *is* alike, she was thinking, taking note of Ray's expensive cabin trunk and dressing case. 'I could do with a cigarette,' she said restlessly, and glancing round for her handbag.

'Here you are, have one of mine,' the other girl offered, pulling out a monogrammed silver case and tossing it on to Rose's bed. 'Where do you go from here?' she asked. 'I mean when the voyage is over.'

'No plans at all — yet. Just glad to be getting out of India.'

'Are you on your own, then? No parents?'

'No,' Rose said. 'And since Mother died it's been no picnic, I can tell you. I've lived in India almost all my life; and for the last five years I've been shifting for myself and paddling my own canoe.'

And only just keeping it afloat, Ray conjectured, staring across at the other girl. There was a kind of spurious smartness about Rose's clothes and belongings; but to Ray, accustomed as

3

she was to the best of everything, one glance was enough. She can't be much more than my age, her thoughts continued as she watched her cabin companion with fascinated curiosity, yet what a lifetime of experience, sordid and otherwise, must lie behind her. But — at least she has *lived*, not like me.

'Come up on deck,' Ray said suddenly, rising uncertainly to her feet. 'Let's see if that stewardess was right.'

Rose got to her feet in one easy fluid movement, and stretched her arms above her head. Well, down and out she may be, Ray thought, observing her, but she is certainly a beauty; and she studied the other girl's pale, clear-cut face with its dark slightly-tilted eyes. Rose's nose was small and delicately aquiline, and her mouth was a pink flower.

'What about you?' Rose asked, as she followed Ray up the companionway to the deck. 'Where do *you* go from here?'

'I'm going back home; at least — ' she smiled slightly, 'to England, where

I'm going to live with a guardian I hardly know. I've lived in the East since the age of seven. My father owned a tile factory near Madras. Ah, this is better!' she broke off to exclaim, stopping and breathing deeply of the fresh salt breeze.

'*And* we seem to have the deck to ourselves,' Rose remarked, looking around her. She pulled forward a couple of chairs. 'You had no job, of course,' she added, looking at Ray.

'Oh, no. There was always plenty of money, and I was an only child. Another thing, I've never been very strong, though I look and feel all right.' Her brown eyes stared out to sea with a curiously strained look about them.

Rose looked at her with interest. 'Well, what happened to change it all?' she asked.

'Both my parents died in a plane crash, and — and — ' She paused, and Rose said:

'You found you had to fend for yourself, eh? Not so much money in the tile factory as you'd thought, eh?'

'Not like that at all,' Ray replied sharply. 'There's plenty of money. But Father left a will and appointed a guardian for me in case I was ever left alone; he must have had a premonition. There are no relatives, you see. I am to make my home with this guardian and his housekeeper. They are old friends of Father's, and the guardian is to administer the estate — that's the expression — till I am twenty-five or till I marry.' Her voice sounded tired, and seemed to hold a bitter note.

Rose gave her another interested look. 'And how old are you now?' she asked.

'Twenty-two — just.'

'Well, that's not long to wait. Gosh, some people have all the luck!'

'Not many people would call it luck to lose one's parents like that,' Ray said, but with a curiously indifferent note in her voice.

'No, of course not; sorry,' Rose said. 'I was thinking of the money.' She clapped her hands sharply at a hovering steward. 'What'll you have to drink, Ray?'

'Er — lime juice and soda, please.'

'Nothing stronger? O.K. Lime juice and soda, and a burra peg for me,' she said to the steward.

'Bit early for that, isn't it?' queried Ray, looking at the sun, which was still well above the horizon. Rose merely stared out to sea, a weary expression suddenly ageing her youthful face. She made no reply.

'When did *your* mother die?' Ray asked, after a short silence.

'Four years ago,' Rose replied, 'and I hardly remember my father. We were in Calcutta at the time; living in a hotel, if you could call it that. Mother was on the stage — sort of — mostly cabaret, and I had been trained for a dancer. I'd had one or two engagements and we weren't doing too badly. Then — she had a stroke. She — she didn't last long after that.' Her voice stopped abruptly, and Ray knew that in spite of her veneer of world-weary toughness Rose had loved her mother and had grieved at her death. 'Well — ' she continued after a brief pause, 'after that I strung along somehow, on my own. I got a few good bookings; money began to flow in — in one way and another. But don't get me wrong,' she added, glancing sideways at Ray with a cynical twist to her lovely mouth. 'Though I had plenty of offers of furnished flats and the Indian equivalent of a mink coat, I managed to steer clear of the lot. None of the gents concerned appealed to me. Fat, middle-aged and married, most of them,' she finished contemptuously.

'What made you decide to come to England?' Ray asked.

Rose was silent again, then she said in a hard voice, 'Oh, I don't know. Yes, I do though. To be honest, I knew that I couldn't really dance; at least, not well enough, I mean, but — well, there was nothing else I could do, and I'd been trained for that. Anyway, the jobs got more sparse, and more squalid, and then — the offers of flats began to be horribly tempting. And so — ' She broke off as the steward approached with the tray of drinks. 'Cheers,' she said to Ray and took a long pull at her glass. 'Ah, that's good! Got another cigarette to give away?' she asked her, as she signed the chit which the steward was offering her, in a scrawling, almost illegible hand. She leaned back again in her chair as Ray took out her lighter and case of cigarettes. There was silence for a moment.

'India's not what it used to be,' Rose remarked presently. 'Since the partition, I mean. There's no place for some of us, even though I wasn't born when it happened.' She paused, then said with a defiant little smile, 'So here I am, penniless, but still — pure.' She grinned again mischievously at Ray who smiled back, for there was something very likeable about this child of fortune; something which forbade pity.

'It — er — surprises me that you are travelling first, then, if you are really down to rock bottom,' Ray said, looking at Rose questioningly.

'Just keeping the old flag flying right to the very last,' Rose said, laughing again. 'I've spent almost my last rupee on this sea trip. I look upon it as the holiday I've never had — before getting down to work.'

'What kind of job will you look for in England?' Ray looked at Rose as she spoke and surprised a look of scared indecision on her face. But it was gone in an instant as she replied almost gaily:

'Well, I'd thought of chorus work — I'm good enough for that — or perhaps teaching; I've got my diploma.'

Ray nodded, but thought at the same time that an Indian diploma would not carry much weight in England where so many girls had ballet training with the appropriate diplomas. But she saw no point in saying this.

'May I join you?' came a masculine voice from behind them, and the two girls looked up to see a dark, thick-set man standing just behind Rose's chair.

Though the deck was still almost deserted, neither of the two girls had seen or heard him approach. Rose recalled now that he was the man who had helped her to locate a piece of baggage on the day the ship sailed. She did not particularly care for his looks, but, after all, he had been helpful, she thought, so now she nodded carelessly.

He promptly drew up a deckchair and sat down close to Rose. Just for a brief moment his eyes turned to Ray as he said, 'May I offer you and your friend another drink?'

Ray hesitated, but Rose, after a casual glance at the newcomer, drawled, 'Thanks, I could do with another. A burra peg for me.'

He turned to Ray, who murmured rather shyly, 'I'd like an orange squash, please.'

The man signalled to a near-by steward and gave the order; then he turned back to his study of Rose's vividly lovely face. 'My name's Trent — Robert Trent,' he said, almost eagerly, waiting for her to show a sign of interest. Rose received this information with complete indifference, and when the drinks arrived, said a brief 'Cheers' and turned again to her contemplation of the horizon.

Ray found herself laboriously carrying on a conversation with a man who had eyes and ears for only Rose.

Much later that same night, as the two girls made ready for bed, Ray said reproachfully, 'Why did you ignore that man Trent? I felt terribly awkward. It wasn't me he wanted to know and talk to, it was you. Did you dislike him, Rose?'

'Oh, he just bored me.'

'Yet you didn't mind taking a drink from him.'

Rose shrugged her shoulders. 'Why not, if he's fool enough to pay for it?' she said.

Ray looked at her with a kind of fascinated disapproval. My, but she's tough, she thought; and was too young and inexperienced to know that this toughness of the other girl had been deliberately cultivated over the years as a protective armour, and was now second nature.

'When were you last in England, Ray?' Rose casually enquired. She stood pulling on pyjama trousers over long slim legs, and Ray took in the perfect modelling of her shoulders and bosom as she reached for the coat. Ray glanced in the mirror at her own rather colourless features and over-slender body. Yet we're the same type, she thought, but — what a difference! There was a sudden silence in the cabin. Rose glanced over her shoulder at her companion, then said sharply, 'I say, d'you feel all right? You look a bit — '

'I'm all right,' Ray interrupted hastily, but rather breathlessly. I get these — turns, occasionally; nothing to worry about. What was it you asked? Oh, yes. Well, I haven't actually *lived* in England since I was six years old; but I have been backwards and forwards several times for short holidays. Originally my parents sent me home to be educated, but I hated it so much, especially the climate, that they brought me back and I went to the Bishop Cotton's schools.' She laughed. 'I must have been a spoilt brat or they'd have insisted on my sticking it out in England. Rose — ' she broke off to ask, 'have you noticed that our stories are rather alike — in general, I mean?' Rose stared at her in surprise. 'Both about the same age, both brought up in India, and now both of us going to England at the same time. See what I mean?'

'Glad you said 'in general',' Rose replied with a mirthless laugh. 'Now, in detail it's quite a different story. I can well imagine the pampered and sheltered life you have led. Everything done for you by bearers and ayahs — in fact, the precious only child of the burrasahib and his memsahib. Now take me — ' She stared over at Ray with narrowed eyes. 'Father — worked on the railways, a poor white, and the less said about him the better. He died of drink. Mother — well — ' She shrugged her shoulders. '*I* was just dragged up, though she did her best, trailing from one cheap Eurasian boarding-house to another even cheaper and nastier. And then, from the age of eighteen, just kicking around on my own, a poor near-white gutter-snipe.'

Ray stared at her in horror. 'Oh, Rose, you must be exaggerating,' she said at last. 'D'you know, I'm beginning to think you just love to dramatise yourself and everything.'

An unexpected dimple appeared in Rose's ivory cheek.

'How right you are,' she said, and burst out laughing.

'In general, I mean. But honestly, my life has been pretty tough, especially the last few years. However, let's skip that near flight of fancy and go on about yourself. How do you feel *now* about going to England?'

Ray sat on the side of her bed. 'I — don't quite know,' she said slowly.

'It's a queer feeling I have, Rose. You see, I'm going to a guardian I hardly know and whom I haven't seen for seven years. I have no relatives at all, and only very sketchy recollections of England.' Her voice stopped and she stared at Rose who was sitting on her bed now with her knees drawn up to her chin. There was a pause, then Rose asked:

'This guardian of yours. Is he to hold the purse-strings, or can you get cracking now with your own plans?'

'Ah, that's just the snag,' Ray replied in a queerly breathless sort of voice. 'My father and mother hedged me round so all my life because I was — delicate, till I almost had no will of my own. Sometimes I felt suffocated with love and care, but it was no use rebelling. And now, in this will, Mr Stanton, the guardian, has full control for the next three years or till I marry; and it's going to be the same story all over again. I shall be hedged around, and — and, oh, life won't be worth living. I *know* that Father wrote and told him all about me, so — ' Her voice ended on a despairing note.

'Queer sort of will,' Rose commented, lighting up a last cigarette. 'Sounds as if your old man couldn't — er — trust you to, well, behave sensibly, sort of thing.'

'No, it was not like that.' Ray's voice was low and tense. 'It's — it's my heart. Any kind of excitement or stimulus results in a condition known as tachycardia. The heart-beats get quicker and quicker, and, well, you see, I have to take things easy — all the time. Day after day, week after week, month after month. Can you imagine what it's like, Rose? But of course you can't. Well, it became an obsession with Daddy. I must not do this, I must not do that, I must not do *anything*. If I wanted a cigarette I had to smoke it on the sly.' Her voice rose hysterically, and Rose murmured:

'Take it easy, take it easy now.' There was silence in the small cabin except for the sound of Ray's hurried, uneven breathing.

'I know,' she said at last, 'but can you imagine what my life has been like? Just dull routine, every day exactly like the one before — in case the slightest change was bad for my heart — and so on — *ad infinitum*. And now I'm afraid it's going to begin all over again. Oh God, if only I could escape!'

'Well,' Rose said, her voice carefully casual as she glanced quickly at the other girl, 'I suppose if your heart's like that, Ray — er — well, you don't want to be blotted out suddenly, do you?'

Ray sprang to her feet and crossed to the other bed. 'I don't believe it's all that bad,' she said restlessly. 'Anyway, Rose, this awful hedged-in life and the continual frustration can't be good for any heart, can it?' She sat sideways on Rose's bed and stared into her face almost imploringly. 'Rose,' she whispered tensely, 'I *must* live, I tell you. I simply *must* break through this stifling net which is *slowly* killing me. Why, I'd

18

far rather *live*, if only for a short time, than this, this — well, wouldn't you? Oh, Rose, if you only knew how much I envy you. Yes, I thought that would surprise you.'

Rose drew thoughtfully on her cigarette, then suddenly burst out laughing. 'Isn't life bloody?' she enquired of the other rather bewildered girl. 'Now, I'd give almost anything for all the comfort and ease — and, yes, all that lovely lolly you have, or are going to have, because I'm so damned tired and sick to death of fending for myself, and being kicked around; while you, it seems, would give anything to fling it all on one side — just to be able to be yourself, to really live and feel *something*, for however short a time. Is that what you want?'

'Yes, yes, that's it, exactly.' Ray's voice was hard.

'If only I could think of a way, Rose. But when I think of the job I had to persuade this guardian to let me travel to England alone, and by boat — ' She sighed and shook her head. 'And even then I doubt if I would have pulled it off if something hadn't happened in his job to make it practically impossible for him to get away.'

'What about the wife; couldn't he have sent her?'

'His wife? Oh, Mr Stanton is a widower now. You see, Rose, I thought that, having several weeks to myself, on this voyage I mean, I might be able to think of a — a plan to get away before it's too late.' Her voice trailed away.

Rose noded her head, then said slowly, 'You said that the cash comes to you in three years' time, or when you marry. Right? Well, Ray, the obvious thing is to concentrate on marriage, isn't it? That's if you are in a hurry to get your hands on this money. Got a boy friend?'

Ray shook her head. 'I've had one or two,' she said slowly, 'but — ' She shrugged her shoulders. 'Well, they just faded out somehow. I guess my father scared them off. And I expect it will be the same old story with this guardian man. What I really want, Rose, is to get away from all the coddling, and all the barriers that are set up. I'm not terribly interested in marrying — not yet. You see, I — I want to be myself; I want to be free of everyone.' She paused and looked at the other girl. 'D'you understand?'

Rose nodded, but was obviously thinking of something else. 'This guardian of yours,' she began, 'what age would he be?'

Ray looked at her in surprise. 'Oh, I don't know,' she said, 'somewhere about Daddy's age, I should think, as they were old friends. Fiftyish, perhaps.'

'A susceptible age for men,' Rose remarked knowledgably as she stubbed out her cigarette end. 'Yes, that's the line you should take, Ray, or — ' She paused, then added thoughtfully, 'Well — perhaps not. You're so very — inexperienced, aren't you?'

But Ray was obviously not with her. 'If I could only think of a way,' she said, 'to get free of it all; get a job of some kind. Then I'd have some fun without being watched all the time; I'd meet men, men of my own choosing, and — and — ' Her voice trailed away once more.

'Well, go to bed and sleep on it,' Rose suggested, thinking to herself: what kind of a job could this girl land with no training or experience of any kind. 'Really, Ray, your best plan is to get to work on this guardian. Soften him up and then it'll be easy to get what you want from him — and three years will soon pass.'

Ray smiled weakly. 'That'd be fine for you, Rose,' she said. 'You've had experience at managing men of all ages, I suppose, and — well, I don't seem to have the same effect on men as you have.'

'Oh, rot. You just think it over, and don't get so worked up. It can't be good for that — '

'Oh, stop, stop,' Ray almost screamed. 'Don't *you* start, for heaven's sake. I've had to put up with that sort of thing all my life, and — oh, I wish I had never told you!' And she jumped up and threw herself on to her own bed.

Rose slid down on to her back. 'I'm sorry, Ray,' she said more gently. 'Look, go to sleep now, and we'll talk it over tomorrow. Between us we'll think of a plan, I'm sure. I do realise how you must feel, and I'll do everything I can to help, truly I will.'

'Oh, that's all right.' Ray's voice was tired and depressed. 'I'm sorry if I got all — melodramatic. I'll try not to think about it — till tomorrow. Good night.'

But the next day she said nothing to Rose on the subject and the latter concluded that she was perhaps turning things over in her mind before bringing it up again. Privately she hoped that Ray had forgotten all about it.

That evening there was a dance in the ship's big ballroom. Rose and Ray went along after dinner and were immediately surrounded by young men. Ray looked round at the animated, ever-moving scene with bright eyes and heightened colour, and when one of Rose's partners said something to her about her 'sister' she stared at him in surprise, then turned to look at Ray who was also dancing, and dancing very well, too, Rose noticed, with a professional eye. Yes, we do look rather alike, she thought, and then hoped with a slight feeling of unease that the other girl was not overdoing things. But her sympathy for Ray's story kept her silent on the subject, and the evening ended with both girls looking bright-eyed and animated as they made for their cabin and bed.

Rose quickly undressed and was brushing out her long dark hair before the mirror when Ray said, all smiles:

'Gosh! It was fun tonight, wasn't it, Rose?'

The latter turned from the mirror and looked down at her. Ray's face was flushed with unusual colour and her eyes were big and glowing. She looks really pretty, Rose thought, and hoped fervently that the other girl had not overtired that heart of hers.

'How I wish life was always like that,' Ray added, 'instead of — ' She paused, and Rose said, turning back to the mirror:

'Yes, it was a whale of an evening. And there'll be more for you to enjoy.'

Ray leaned sideways to pick up her handbag. In taking something from it she also pulled out her passport. It fell to the floor with the photograph page uppermost.

'What's your photo like?' Rose asked idly, bending to pick up the passport. 'They're usually good for a laugh. I say!' she exclaimed after a slight pause. 'They certainly did you proud. This is a super effort; worth enlarging, in my opinion.'

Ray laughed in a pleased fashion as she got up and leaned over Rose's shoulder.

'It flatters me really,' she said, looking down at the small picture. Suddenly she turned her head and stared into Rose's face. 'Looks more like you than me,' she said, 'it does really. They've made the hair and eyes darker. See what I mean?'

Rose glanced again at the picture and nodded. 'They often do in photos,' she remarked. 'Over-exposed, I expect. Mine's pretty awful. Like to have a dekko?' And she flicked her own passport over in Ray's direction.

'Yes, it certainly doesn't do you justice — a typical P.P. picture.' Ray's voice was thoughtful; and as Rose looked at her there was a queerly calculating expression on her face. 'Could be — anyone really, could even be — me,' she added, laughing.

Rose echoed her laughter, then got to her feet after pushing the passport back into her handbag. 'Ready to doss down?' she asked. 'I certainly am.'

But Ray was standing now and staring in front of her.

'Come on,' Rose said impatiently. 'I want some sleep even if you don't.'

Ray sat down slowly again on the side of her bed. 'Rose,' she said, a note of intense excitement in her voice, 'I've

26

thought of a plan.'

Rose did not pretend to misunderstand. She'd hoped that Ray had solved her problem in her own way; and now perhaps she had. 'Well, what is it?' she enquired rather wearily, for it was getting very late.

Ray stared at her for a long moment in a kind of pulsing silence, then she gave a breathless little laugh, and said, 'Rose — I — I'll be — you; and you'll — be me.'

2

Slowly, Rose turned from the mirror and stared at the other girl in amazement. 'What the hell do you mean?' she said. 'I be you, and you be me! Be your own age at least and talk sense. Come on, Ray, out with it. What mad idea is in your head now?'

'Well — ' Ray's voice was jerky with excitement. 'You said you'd give anything to have my circumstances, and money — and I — well, if I could change places with you, I could live, really live, couldn't I?'

'More likely starve,' Rose interrupted roughly. 'Oh, don't talk — '

'But, Rose, don't you see? Why shouldn't we exchange identities? It could be done — easily. The passports gave me the idea. Just think — '

Rose stood there, straight and slim in her skimpy cotton pyjamas and stared at Ray. Her big dark eyes were wide and still, and her flower mouth hung open. 'Ray,' she whispered, 'are you mad? That's the craziest idea I've ever had to listen to. Why, it's — it's — well, it's mad. It just is not possible.'

'Think,' Ray urged again in a hoarse whisper, 'and you'll see that it *is* possible. Just think for a minute, Rose. We're almost the same age, we *could* look alike; like enough to exchange passports, anyway, and get away with it. We are both going to England where no one really knows either of us; my guardian won't remember what I looked like at thirteen. We know about each — '

'Stop, stop, Ray,' and Rose suddenly burst out laughing. 'My poor girl, you must be plain crackers. Why, apart from anything else, *you* couldn't last five minutes on your own. You've never had to rely on your own efforts. How could *you* earn a living, or — ?'

'But don't you see, I'd be you — Rose Delmont — and I *can* act and dance, and — '

'Oh, shut up, Ray,' Rose interrupted in exasperation. 'I think it's your head that's cracked, not your heart. I don't want to hear any more.' And she banged down the hairbrush and climbed into bed.

'But, Rose, wouldn't you love to have lots of money, beautiful clothes, live in lovely surroundings? Wouldn't you love to step off this boat as the rich Miss Ray Desmond, instead of — ?'

'The rich Miss Ray Desmond,' Rose interrupted. 'Oh, yes, the rich Miss Ray Desmond whose purse-strings are held firmly by dear guardian; who is hedged in and around, and who can't call her soul her own, and — '

'But, Rose — ' Ray cut in again. 'Rose dear, *you* understand men; you'd soon twist things your own way. It would be an easy matter for you with all *your* experience. Rose — ' her voice dropped to a beguiling whisper, 'wouldn't you *love* to walk off the gangway at Southampton — ' There was a moment's tense silence, then Rose said:

'Yes, I would, of course I would. And so would you, if you'd had my life for the last five years, but — but not this way, thanks. Oh, I wish you'd shut up, Ray; I suppose this is your idea of a joke, but I just don't appreciate your sense of humour.'

'But — I'm not joking, you see. I really am desperate to break free and live a life of my own; however short and whatever the cost. You are equally desperate to — '

'Hey, just a minute. Where did you get that impression from? I'm not as desperate as all that. There are plenty of things I can do to make a living. No, you're crazy, Ray. *Good* night.' And Rose reached up and switched off the light.

There was a vibrating sort of silence as Ray also got into bed and switched off her side light. Then — 'Think it over, Rose,' came in a soft whisper from the darkness.

'Shut up, can't you?' But though Rose closed her eyes, and tried to close her ears, she could not close her mind to this crazy but subtly tempting proposition. Try as she would, after a short while her galloping imagination took control, and one tempting picture after another floated before her closed eyes.

Ray's plan *could* be carried through, Rose saw that. In fact, the whole thing seemed almost as if it had been arranged for them. They had not been on the ship long enough for anyone to be sure of names; even to the purser and stewardess they were merely Miss Desmond and Miss Delmont, two girls of about the same age in cabin forty-nine.

Suddenly Rose saw herself behind the wheel of a super sports car; then floating round the Dorchester ballroom in a Mary Quant gown; climbing the steps of a plane for a weekend in Paris. Attending a fashion parade and nonchalantly putting her signature to the purchase of unbelievably beautiful dresses, swimsuits and lingerie. She gritted her teeth and desperately attempted to throttle the next flight of fancy which this time centred in the hunting field with herself on a mettlesome chestnut mare, in spite of the fact that all Rose had ridden so far were hill ponies and 'cast' Army mounts. But this did not prevent her from clearing five-barred gates and leading the whole field to the 'kill'. Rose was just sinking, exhausted, into an uneasy sleep when the soft whisper came again. 'There's a this year's Jaguar waiting for you, Rose.'

She flung herself out of bed, and said violently into the darkness, 'Ray, I'll strangle you, heart or no heart, if you don't shut up and leave me alone. I'm no saint, as you very well know; but what you suggest is wrong and dishonest. But apart from that, *you* could never pull it off, you're not tough enough. You just couldn't take it — and you might — yes, die any day. Now do you see why I couldn't ever — ever?'

'Rose.' Ray switched on the light and sat up. She snatched at the other girl's hand, and Rose noticed uneasily how hot and clammy hers was. 'But don't you see? That's just it — the key to it all. I must — I tell you I *must* get free — before — '

Rose dropped to her knees before the other bed. 'Look, Ray,' she said, and her voice was now very gentle and quiet. 'Ray dear, please be sensible. Your idea is quite, quite impossible. Try to see it from my point of view. My suggestion is the one to work on, softening up the guardian, I mean. Would you like me to come with you to meet him, and perhaps together we could talk to him and persuade him to — to, well, let you have a shot at living your own life. I'd be quite willing to help you once I've got myself started, and if, as you say, you can really dance and act, well — let's give it a trial anyway. You know, I'm sure you could do this thing gradually, and — anyway, why throw away all your advantages of money and the rest?'

'Oh well, perhaps you're right.' Ray's

voice was suddenly very tired and flat as she slumped back on to her pillows. 'I suppose it was a mad idea. But I still don't see why *you* — '

'Not again, please, Ray. Put it right out of your mind and concentrate on *my* plan,' and she gave the hand she still held a strong comforting squeeze before going back to her own bed.

A few hours later Rose woke once more. She shivered suddenly and thought the cabin seemed very cold — and empty. With a vague feeling of unease she switched on the side light and looked across at the other bed. Ray was lying on her back and sleeping peacefully, and Rose drew a deep breath of relief. She lay down again and was about to switch off the light when something made her glance across once more at the opposite bed. Then, Rose raised herself sharply on her elbow and her heart gave a sickening thump. Ray's face! There was a queer bluish tinge about it. Rose had not noticed at first glance, but now it showed up against the whiteness of the pillow. Sweat broke out on her forehead, but she forced herself to climb out of her bed and approach the other.

'Ray,' Rose whispered, and laid a shrinking hand on the other girl's shoulder; but as soon as her hand was in contact with the naked flesh she knew the awful frightening truth. *Ray was dead*. Rose's teeth began to chatter. She drew back, then stumbled with trembling limbs towards the bell push. But, as she stretched out a cold hand, she hesitated. Something inside herself, some vague memory from the previous night, seemed to hold her back. 'Don't ring the bell — yet,' the something whispered. 'Now's your chance, Rose Delmont. You would not have done it while she was alive — you told her so — but now — ' Rose's ice-cold hand crashed hard against her white lips.

'Stop it, stop it,' she gasped sound-lessly; but the whisper came again. 'You won't be harming Ray — or anyone.

She's dead — and she was an only child — someone might as well have all that — '

'No, no, I must *not*.'

'Go on, you fool, don't miss this chance; you'll never have another like it — she offered, no, implored you, to take her place.'

'Oh no, no. God, don't let me!'

'All that money, a life of ease — everything you've always wanted; just waiting to be picked up. What is waiting for *you* in England? Just nothing; you don't know a soul, and — go on, Rose, don't be a fool. Go on, it won't take a minute to change passports, handbags, suitcases — '

As in a trance Rose turned, swaying slightly, her cold hand dropping nervelessly to her side. She paused for a second, gave a kind of half-sob — and moved swiftly back to the dead girl's side.

When the stewardess knocked on the door in response to the long ring, a faint agitated voice called, 'Oh, come in, please, come in. I think — I think — ' and Rose broke into a torrent of tears. The woman rushed across the room and her eyes went at once to the still figure on the bed and then to the other crouched by it.

'What is the matter?' she asked, and put a hand on Rose's shoulder. 'Is Miss Delmont ill?' and she peered closely at the still face on the pillow, then slipped a hand under the thin silk nightdress.

'I couldn't wake her,' whispered Rose, raising a white strained face. 'I was afraid,' and she broke down again, the tears streaming down her face.

'Now, don't upset yourself, dear,' said the stewardess. 'I'll fetch the doctor at once. Put your dressing-gown on, and try to pull yourself together, there's a good girl,' and as she bustled out of the cabin Rose thought to herself, with surprised confusion: these are real tears, not just hysteria; I really liked Ray! Then another thought came, a stealthy thought. The stewardess had referred to the dead girl as Miss

Delmont. It was almost as if fate intended that this exchange of identity should take place. Rose shivered violently, and found that she could not stop, and could not look at Ray's still face. It was not too late even now, she thought distractedly. She could put back the passports; she *would* put them back. Frantically she began to scramble to her feet; but then — Rose's head began to swim. And when the doctor and the stewardess hurried in they found her slumped on the floor in a faint.

She opened her eyes at the sound of a man's voice. 'How is Miss Desmond now, Stewardess?' she heard him say. 'Has she come round yet? Ah, I see she has. Good.' And Rose saw a kind, elderly face bending over her. 'I'm going to give you a sedative, my dear,' he said, smiling reassuringly. 'You have had a nasty shock. But first, tell me what happened.'

Rose struggled weakly to sit up, but he pressed her gently back. 'No, no, lie down,' he said. 'I want you just to tell me exactly what happened.'

'Nothing — nothing happened,' she said in a flat voice. 'I — I just woke up — and suddenly the cabin seemed very quiet — too quiet, and — ' Her throat worked as she made a painful effort to remain calm; but through it all Rose noted with a kind of fatalism that the doctor had also called her 'Miss Desmond'. 'Then I switched on the light,' she continued, 'and — and she looked queer, and — and I couldn't wake her; and — she was so cold.' Rose put an arm over her eyes. 'That's all. Then I rang the bell.' She drew a long shuddering breath, and there was silence.

'Don't upset yourself, Miss Desmond. We'll have to ask you a few more questions, but not now. Drink this, my dear,' and he held a glass to Rose's lips. She drank the mixture and in a short while slid gently into oblivion. Her last coherent thought was, 'Must do something about the passports; or — is it too late?'

When Rose wakened from her drugged sleep she saw at once that she was in a different cabin; with nothing in it to remind her of the recent tragedy. All Ray's belongings were stacked neatly round, but there was no sign of her own. Her handbag — no, it was Ray's — was beside her on the bedside table. Rose opened it with cold fingers and drew out the passport. Slowly she opened it and stared fascinated at Ray's pictured face. The stewardess came in and smiled brightly at her.

'How are you feeling, dear?' she asked. 'Well enough to answer a few questions?' Rose nodded, knowing that it had to be gone through. The woman hesitated, and Rose saw that she was preparing to help her to dress.

'I can manage on my own,' she said, for she needed to collect her thoughts; and also to choose clothes which would fit her from Ray's wardrobe. The dead girl had been slighter in build than herself and Rose knew she would have to be careful. She wanted no witnesses.

Within a few minutes the stewardess returned and conducted a still slightly comatose Rose along endless passages and through doors to what she supposed were the captain's quarters. It had seemed to Rose as she walked jerkily along that the floors were becoming increasingly unsteady, and she was not surprised when she heard a passing steward remark, 'We're in for some dirty weather, I guess.'

'Sit down, Miss Desmond.' The captain had a thin, brown face and silvery hair. 'I hope you feel equal to answering a few necessary questions, but first, drink this coffee — it will do you good.' Rose did as she was told, and he continued: 'Now, how much can you tell us of the dead girl? I see. Had she confided in you at all? Had she spoken to you of her health? Did she speak to you of any relatives, or friends? Had she — '

And so the questions went on and on, and Rose heard her own voice replying. No, she knew very little of

42

— her. They had been strangers to each other when they boarded the ship at Bombay. She knew, however, that the other girl had no relatives anywhere. The heart trouble had been mentioned, but the dead girl had not seemed to take it seriously.

Suddenly the cabin floor seemed to rise then fall away — and Rose fainted once more.

The bad weather lasted for several days, and though Rose, who was one of the world's worst sailors, suffered, it did at least give her time to collect herself. She was now committed to this deception, and having taken the final step she now quite calmly and almost naturally stepped into Ray's shoes. Of course, her stage training helped her. She found everything surprisingly easy, and when the weather abated and she was able to go up on deck she found that so much was taken for granted by those around her that she had little to do or say. In fact, Rose found that this deception she had started went on almost by itself.

Rather surprisingly, her sorrow for Ray was real. Poor kid, she'd had so little, Rose thought, then smiled wryly at the incongruity of it.

She thought it best now to discourage all attempts at friendship or sympathy, and Rose had to be very firm with the swarthy Mr Trent, who tried hard to establish himself as her constant companion. Several times she caught him looking at her in a queer sort of way, and one evening, catching her alone on a quiet part of the promenade deck, he said to her:

'D'you know, Miss — Desmond, I could have sworn that it was the other girl whose name was Ray.'

'Really?' Rose said coolly. 'But then, you hardly knew her — or me, did you?' and turned away from him.

'Well, what's it matter, anyway?' he said in a low tone, and following Rose. 'We can always remedy that, can't we?' and she felt his arm sliding furtively round her waist.

Rose stopped, then brought the side of her hand down sharply on to his forearm. 'I have no desire for it to be remedied,' she said, and turned contemptuously away, and as she did so she heard him muttering furiously under his breath. But later, in the privacy of her cabin, Rose wondered if she had been wise to antagonise this man. She remembered the look in his eyes and knew she had made an enemy.

As the days slipped by Rose's conscience troubled her less and less as her imagination pictured the life ahead of her. But sometimes, particularly in the dark nights, doubt and terror assailed her. Sooner or later, someone, perhaps a childhood friend of the dead girl, perhaps an old friend of her parents, even a very distant relative, might turn up, and then she would need all her wits. But then, Rose thought, hadn't she lived by her wits most of her life? And hadn't the dead girl herself wanted it this way?

At last the fatal hour arrived. The

ship docked in the early morning. Rose dressed herself carefully, then took a last long scrutiny of Ray's passport, now of course her own. She had dressed her hair in the exact style of the picture and tried to remember to compress her full lips to a slightly thinner line.

Her baggage had already been taken out by the cabin steward, and now Rose was ready to take up her handbag and dressing case and make her way to the saloon where the Port Authorities were checking the passengers' papers and passports.

Rose looked round the cabin, and gave a last thought to the girl who had died so tragically. With a sudden stab of dread she realised how very little she really knew about this girl. Rose had never been able to bring herself to ask what had had to be done — after that terrifying night; she wanted desperately to forget it all. She caught a fleeting glimpse of herself in the mirror. Her face was pale and her eyes looked haunted.

This is it, she told herself fiercely. From now on, you must not only look like Ray, and talk like Ray. You've got to *think* like her, too. In fact, you've got to be Ray — from now on. So — it's up to you — Ray Desmond. She drew a long trembling breath, then with firm steps and head held high Rose walked out of her cabin, along the white passage-way, up the steps and into the crowded saloon.

She was calm and composed as she looked about her; but beneath the smart red tailored suit she was wearing Rose's heart was beating so rapidly and heavily that it seemed to her that it must be audible. She passed her tongue over suddenly-dry lips, then jumped nervously as a man's voice behind her said:

'You are Miss Ray Desmond, aren't you?'

'Y-yes,' Rose said, turning round slowly. Into her mind had slid the thought: 'This is the first spoken lie. Oh, I wish, I wish' — and she raised her eyes to the face of the man who stood there watching her. Rose looked straight into a pair of the bluest eyes she had ever seen; and her heart gave a quick, almost painful leap. The two pairs of eyes, one brown, one blue, gazed at each other for a soundless moment. 'Who is this man?' Rose wondered, then: 'Oh no, no, it can't be.' For, for some reason, the obvious answer to her question was queerly frightening.

3

'My name is Drake; Laurie Drake,' said the owner of the very blue eyes. 'Mr Stanton — your guardian — asked me to meet you as he was unable to meet you himself.' He looked at Rose and smiled. 'He asked me to make his apologies. May I help you with your passport and papers? I hope it won't take too long. Do you feel up to it, or shall I — ?'

'Oh no, that's O.K., Mr Drake, I can manage. Thank you very much for coming to meet me.' She gave the young man her brilliant, casual smile, and he blinked in a slightly surprised fashion.

'Well — let me help you, anyway,' he said. 'Shall we join the queue?'

Rose smiled and nodded. She was very glad that this nice, attractive man was not the guardian she was all set to deceive. He was too young anyway, she thought suddenly, and — her eyes slid sideways, and she saw that he was watching her with frank, unmistakeable admiration. Rose's heart gave an excited jerk, and a faint blush warmed the pallor of her cheeks. She felt happy all at once, happy and exhilarated; yet, at the same time, another feeling, unwelcome but annoyingly persistent, was struggling to come to life under the smart white pure silk blouse she was wearing. She shrugged her shoulders impatiently, then gave a short laugh. It amused Rose to think that she, Rose Delmont, the girl tough who had been paddling her own precarious canoe ever since childhood, should now be acting like a susceptible schoolgirl; and all because of an anxious-looking young man with blue eyes and a nice smile.

'Look,' Rose said abruptly, turning to her companion, 'I can manage these,' she flicked at the papers and passport, 'if you will round up my cases and see them ashore to the Customs. There they are,' and she waved a hand towards a pile of expensive-looking suitcases near the door.

'Yes — all right,' he said, turning away; but not before Rose had seen again the expression of surprise in his blue eyes. She realised all at once that she was not playing the part of a delicate, sheltered girl at all well. Of course, he would not be expecting her to be independent and self-reliant at all. Robert Stanton would have told him that she was something of an invalid and would expect to be looked after. The thought brought Rose up with a jerk. The implications were vaguely unwelcome, and for the first time she wondered uneasily if she had undertaken more than she could cope with. This man, too, Laurie Drake — he made Rose forget about the ill-fated Ray. His blue eyes were so clear and candid. Beside him Rose suddenly felt like a cardboard figure, with no substance and no inner meaning; and all at once she wanted desperately to be herself. Then into her mind swam thoughts of the lovely, easy, affluent future. It'll work out, she told herself impatiently, of course it will, everything's going to be fine.

When she joined Laurie Drake on the deck a few minutes later Rose gave him an appealing little-girl smile, and allowed him to take charge of everything.

'Be careful how you walk down the gangway,' he advised, then took Rose's arm as they made their way to the Customs shed. Here he insisted on her sitting down on a convenient box while he moved cases up and down on to the tables, unlocked and locked them, and, in fact, completed the tiring task of clearing the Customs.

After it was all over, Laurie took Rose's arm again and led her to the dock gates, where a shabby but roomy red Austin car awaited them.

'You get in, Miss Desmond,' he said, opening the car door, 'while I stow away the cases. It will be a bit of a squeeze, but we'll manage, I think.'

'Thank you,' Rose murmured.

She gave a little shiver, and he asked at once, 'Are you cold?' Without waiting for an answer, he pulled a rug from the back seat. 'Let me tuck this round you,' he said, then laughed gently. 'Of course, you are not used to the rigours of the English summers, are you?'

Rose shook her head smilingly, and looked at his crisp, springy, light-brown hair as he bent over her. 'No, it's quite a long time since I was in England,' she observed, and was glad that at least that was not a lie, as she *had* visited England when a small child. He spread the rug carefully over her knees, then went round to the back of the car.

Laurie packed away all Rose's cases, then climbed in beside her. Before starting the engine he turned to her again and made certain that she was well wrapped up; and Rose became conscious of a very strange, unaccustomed feeling : that of being cared for and cherished. It was a feeling she had not had since very early childhood, and then for a brief time only. Now, she relaxed and sighed happily. It was a pleasant feeling, she thought, very pleasant indeed; but it did not last for long. She was conscious again of that — something; that uncomfortable something that was still struggling inside her. Angrily, Rose tried to stifle it. She turned with excited interest to the unfamiliar country through which they were passing. Green hedgerows, fields of green, green grass, small sheets of silvery water, woods with every shade of green stretching up the gentle hill slopes. All the colours were soft and indefinite and merged imperceptibly from one into the other.

Rose thought all at once of the vast country she had left. Its monotonously long, narrow, dust-covered roads; the dingy mud villages sprawled under the sparse shade of the inevitable neem tree; the bare, rocky slopes of the hills, barren and brown; the harsh contrasts of light and shade; and a queer nostalgia came over her. It is my country, she thought. I wonder if I shall ever see it again. Perhaps — later. She turned to the man beside her, and saw that he was quietly enjoying her own evident interest and excitement.

'What a lovely country!' Rose said. 'Is it like this where — Mr Stanton lives?'

'Yes. Hampshire and Surrey are very much alike, and Farndon is on the borders of the two. Have you been looking forward to coming home, Miss Desmond?'

'I — don't quite know,' she said. 'You see, I have lived in South India nearly all my life, and — well, I can't yet think of England as — home.'

'Of course, I can quite understand that,' Laurie Drake said, watching Rose's lovely profile. 'But — I do hope you will be happy here, and if there is ever anything I can do — ' he smiled at her, then added rather shyly, 'Perhaps you will let me show you something of the country after you have settled in?'

'Why, yes, of course,' Rose replied,

pleasure catching at her breath. 'It's very kind of you, Mr Drake. I shall look forward to it.'

'My name is Laurie,' he said suddenly. He turned and smiled at her, a question in his eyes. But Rose hesitated, then looked away. She could not ask this nice man to call her by her name, and equally, for some unacknowledged reason, she would not ask him to call her by the name of the dead girl. So she was silent, and after a short pause he looked straight ahead and began to talk on impersonal things.

Rose sighed impatiently. She knew Laurie would regard it as a snub, but was not yet prepared to do anything about it. After all, she thought, she must not let this quite nice young man complicate her new life. She knew nothing about him and — there was plenty of time.

The sun was just setting as the car turned in at the gates of a large half-timbered house with a sweep of green lawn in front.

'Well, here we are,' Rose's companion said. He looked at her anxiously. 'I do hope the journey hasn't tired you too much, Miss Desmond.'

'Good Lord, no,' Rose said impatiently and without thinking. 'Why ever should — ' and then she stopped. Of course, her heart. She made an abrupt movement with her shoulders. This was going to be a continual nuisance, Rose thought, and wondered again, and with an increased sense of dismay, just what the future held, and whether she could really manipulate it her *way*. 'I've got to,' she thought fiercely, 'otherwise where is all this taking me, and what was the point of — ?' She broke off her thoughts and turned to Laurie. 'I — have enjoyed the ride,' Rose said quietly.

An elderly woman in a black dress opened the door and smiled at Rose, and at the same moment a door on the right of the large square hall opened, and a tall man came out. He looked at Rose, and for a split second she saw the amazement in his eyes before he hurried up with outstretched hand.

'Welcome, my dear Ray,' he said, and bent to kiss her cheek.

Rose was at a loss for words. This man was not at all what she had expected; and she had a good idea that she was not what he had expected, either. For one thing, he was much younger. She looked up into Robert Stanton's face. 'Why, he's not old at all,' Rose thought, and wondered why the fact half-excited, half-dismayed her, but she smiled at him and replied to his greeting.

He drew her over to a chair, and she noticed that he was taller than Laurie Drake. He had thick, dark brown hair, beginning to go grey at the temples, and his eyes were a very clear, very light grey — rather striking, Rose thought.

'Come along in, Ray,' Robert Stanton said heartily.

'This is Mrs Branksome, my house-keeper. We are just going to have tea. Come over to the fire.'

Rose smiled again and murmured a greeting as the elderly woman rustled away.

'Did you enjoy the ride up?' Robert Stanton continued, and slid an arm affectionately over Rose's shoulders. He led her towards the open door, talking all the time. 'I was sorry I could not come along to meet you myself, but I had a very important consultation which it was impossible to delegate to someone else or to postpone. I hope Drake looked after you well. Come and join us in a cup of tea,' he said over his shoulder to the younger man. Rose studied his face as he bent forward and plumped up a chair cushion. Yes, he looks just what he is, she thought, someone exclusive and brainy. For Ray had told her that the guardian was a well-known medical research chemist.

'Mr Drake looked after me very well,' she murmured, trying to catch his eye past Stanton's broad shoulder. 'He made the trip very interesting for me.'

'Good,' was the reply. 'Well — sit

down, Ray. Here is Mrs Branksome with the tea, and I am sure you can do with a cup.'

Rose sank down into the comfortable chair and looked about her. It was a large, lofty room, tastefully furnished, and with quite costly pictures and ornaments about; not that Rose knew a great deal about such things, but her naturally good taste told her so. But even so, there was something missing, she thought. The room had a faint air of neglect. Not exactly ill-cared for; the furniture was glossy and free from dust. It was rather as if everything had been there for a little too long. The bronze curtains were rich and heavy, but slightly faded in the folds. The edge-to-edge Wilton carpet was just a little worn in places. The upholstery of the chairs and couches was expensive but far from new. Perhaps it's since his wife died, Rose thought, because Ray did say that he was well-off. For the first time she suddenly wondered what Robert Stanton thought about a grown-up young woman invading his home for an indefinite period. However, she concluded, he did not seem to mind, and — if *I* have my way it won't be for very long. Twenty-five, Ray had said, or before if she married. Well, that shouldn't be difficult, Rose thought, for I'll get the opportunities at last of meeting the kind of man I want to marry. A man of wealth, culture and class who would be able to lift her for ever from the — no, it had not been the gutter, not quite; but, and Rose shivered suddenly, sometimes it had been uncomfortably near. But now, the future loomed bright, even if she did not marry. In three years' time, or slightly less, she would have all that money to do with as she would. Rose's heart began to beat with exultation as she contemplated all the lovely things she would buy, the places she would visit, the things she would do.

Rose came out of her daydreams at the rattle of a teatray, and her eyes met the clear blue eyes of Laurie Drake. He smiled at her and her heart seemed to swell as she smiled back. It was a queer feeling she had; and Rose could not remember having had it since, as a very young girl, she had risen early one morning just as dawn was breaking, and gone for a swim in the lake at Naini-Tal in Southern India. The dawn sky had been flushed with a swathe of deep rose; there was just the slightest whisper of a breeze from the trees on the bank, and in the middle of the lake some wild geese silently settled on the still water. Rose remembered how she had held her breath at the purity and beauty of it all — and longed for something she could not put a name to. She had never been able to find it, but as she looked into the clear eyes just above her own, Rose knew that she still wanted and longed for this nameless thing.

She blinked and took the cup he was holding out to her, and saw then that Robert Stanton had drawn a chair close to hers. Laurie glanced quietly round, then sat in a chair opposite.

'You are looking extremely well, my dear Ray,' Stanton said, half-turning and looking into her face. 'The voyage must have done you good; but, of course, you must take things easy at first, just till we see how you go on.'

'Yes, of course,' Rose murmured gently, but with her lips setting in a firm line. She looked at him and smiled confidently. 'But I'm perfectly all right, Mr Stanton,' she added. 'My parents fussed over me too much; there was no need. I feel perfectly fit, and have done so for a long time now. My father was the worst. He — '

'Well, perhaps so,' Robert Stanton interrupted. 'But it was for your own good, and they were quite right not to allow you to take risks. No, it's a quiet life for you, I'm afraid, Ray.'

Rose said nothing to this, but as she caught the eye of Laurie Drake he smiled at her gently and encouragingly.

'What will you have to eat, Ray?' Robert Stanton asked, then raised his wrist and looked pointedly at the watch. 'Time you were getting back, isn't it?' he asked the younger man, who rose at once to his feet.

'Yes, it is,' he quietly agreed. 'I am on duty at 'Casualty' tonight. Thanks for the tea. Goodbye, Miss Desmond, and I shall hope to see you again soon.' He smiled at Rose, then crossed to the door.

'Goodbye,' she said. 'And — I shall hope to see *you*, and thanks for bringing me along.' Rose gave him her sudden brilliant smile, and was sorry to see him go.

'Is Mr Drake a doctor?' she asked Mr Stanton as the door closed behind him.

'Yes, he is at the 'General' here. Try one of these sandwiches, Ray, they're rather good.'

'No, thank you, I'm not really hungry — just tired.' 'And suddenly depressed,' she thought. 'I hate this borrowed name.' Then mentally Rose shrugged her shoulders impatiently. What was the matter with her all at once? She had gone into this thing with her eyes open, hadn't she? She had been sick to death of being Rose Delmont, a thing of no account, and with no foreseeable future. She had seized this chance and, with Ray dead, had cheated no one. And Ray herself had wanted it that way, Rose reminded herself again. So what was the matter with her? 'Oh, snap out of it,' she told herself wearily, 'you're getting soft. You haven't committed a crime — well, not really. You just seized an opportunity. And what's wrong with that? Nothing. No one would get anywhere in this world if they didn't grab the opportunities that came along.'

Rose saw that Stanton was watching her with an enigmatic look in his eyes. 'Sure you won't have another cup of tea?' he asked, then, as she shook her head, added, 'I do hope you will be happy here, Ray; you must look upon my house as your home now, and try to forget the unhappy past.' He paused. 'You don't want to talk about it, of course?'

'No, oh no,' Rose said quickly. The less said about her past the better, she thought. 'Thank you for having me here — ' she looked swiftly at him, then away, 'for the time being.'

'Oh, but I am happy to have you here — for always,' he replied, and at a note in his voice Rose glanced quickly again into his light, almost colourless eyes. They gazed back smilingly; yet, without quite knowing why, she looked away from him with a queerly uneasy feeling. 'You see — ' he was beginning again when there was the sound of a door quietly opening. Rose looked towards it in relief as Stanton stood up and called out somewhat impatiently:

'Come in, Alison, come in,' and a little girl of about ten advanced shyly and awkwardly into the room.

'Ray, this is my daughter, Alison,' Robert Stanton said, and Rose only just managed to cloak her glance of startled amazement. This was something Ray had not mentioned; that the guardian had a daughter. How many other facts had she not told her, Rose wondered anxiously.

However, by the time the child had come right up to the chair, Rose had recovered her composure. She smiled in a friendly way at the fair-haired, rather frail-looking little girl, and held out a hand.

'How are you, Alison?' she said. 'I'm very pleased to meet you.' The child smiled shyly but eagerly, and was about to speak when her father cut in briskly:

'Alison will show you to your room, Ray. I expect you would like a rest, wouldn't you? I have to put in some rather urgent work in the laboratory, so — '

4

Languidly, Rose opened her eyes. Her bedroom was full of sunlight. Net curtains fluttered at the half-open casement windows, and the gentle tinkle of china on a tray came pleasantly to her ears.

'Good morning, Miss Desmond,' came a voice, and Rose turned her head to see Mrs Branksome, the house-keeper, looking down at her. 'It's a beautiful day,' she remarked as she set the tray on the bedside table, then crossed over to the window. 'If there is anything you want, please ring.' She twitched at a curtain, then muttered over her shoulder, 'That girl's forgotten to close the shutters again. I hope you weren't cold in the night.'

'No, oh no,' Rose said, and then as the housekeeper went out of the room she sat up and looked about her. In her peach silk nightdress, and with her ruffled black hair and brilliant dark eyes, Rose looked very lovely. Her name suited her; her real name, that is. Drawing a deep breath of delight, Rose's eyes wandered lazily from one object to another. She looked at the soft, ankle-deep carpet, the rose-pink cushions, curtains and chair covers, and the dressing-table with its many mirrors at all angles. Last night she had been too tired and excited with all the new impressions to take it in, but now all her senses were wide awake. Everything in the room was new, she was sure of that. Rose stretched slender arms above her head, revelling in the feeling of luxury and ease. Then into her mind came the memory of other bedrooms she had occupied. Bedrooms in cheap hotel and boardinghouses all over India. Torn matting on the floors, dingy dasuti curtains at the windows. And suddenly she shuddered. 'Forget it,' Rose told herself fiercely. 'It's all over — and now it's up to you, Rose

Delmont — no, Ray Desmond — to see that it stays that way. This is your way of life now. No more wondering about where the next meal or bed is to come from. Oh, this is wonderful!' And she clasped her arms tightly across her breast.

As Rose turned to pour herself a cup of tea from the dainty flowered china at her side she heard a slight sound at the door. Then, as it slowly opened, she saw a small face peering round the edge.

'Ray, may I come in?' Alison asked shyly.

'Of course,' Rose called, and smiled invitingly at the child. She had never had much to do with children, and was not really interested in them. But there was something rather appealing about this one; with her straight fair hair in two neat plaits, and her big grey eyes. Yes, there was something; was it loneliness, Rose wondered, and smiled again at the child. Whatever it was, she now stretched out a hand and drew the little girl near to her.

'How nice of you to come and say

'Good morning' to me,' she said.

Alison's eyes were straying over the peach silk and lace of Rose's nightdress. 'Lovely,' she murmured, drawing a small hand over the smooth surface. Rose laughed, then looked at her wristwatch.

'A quarter to nine!' she exclaimed. 'I had no idea it was so late. Are you just off to school?'

'Oh, no,' Alison's voice sounded quite shocked. 'It's holiday time, didn't you know?'

'No, I'm afraid I didn't. You see, Alison, it's different in India where I have come from. The long school holiday is in October.'

'Why is that — ?' Alison was beginning, but broke off as a bell rang sharply from somewhere downstairs. 'That's for breakfast,' she said. 'I must go now, Ray. Daddy doesn't like me to be late.' She started for the door and Rose said in some dismay:

'Oh dear! I'm afraid I shall be very late indeed.'

'No, no, you're not to get up, Ray,' Alison said urgently from the door. 'Mrs Branksome is to bring yours up, Daddy said. It's because you're not strong,' and with the last words she hurried out of the room.

Rose looked after the child, then shrugged her shoulders. Oh well, it was quite a treat for her to have breakfast in bed; but she resolved that tomorrow she would be up in good time. This invalid business was going to be one hell of a nuisance, she thought, but — and here Rose smiled to herself — she'd soon get things going *her* way. She'd handled many men in her short life, and was sure that she could deal with Robert Stanton.

After breakfast, which the house-keeper brought to her on a tray, Rose spent a breathtaking half-hour unpacking Ray's beautiful garments. She thrust thoughts of the dead girl out of her mind. The house seemed very quiet as she came down the side softly-carpeted stairs, but she heard Alison's voice in the garden and went out to join her. The little girl was on the lawn, throwing a ball for a fat brown spaniel to chase.

'Hello, Ray,' she called, and ran to meet her. 'This is my dog; his name is Lugs. Mr Drake christened him. Isn't it a funny name?'

'Certainly is,' Rose laughed, and strolled forward across the smooth grass. 'But it suits him.' She wondered if Laurie Drake were a frequent visitor at the house.

'Daddy is going to take us out in the car this afternoon,' Alison volunteered eagerly. 'He says you are to choose where we shall go. Oh, can we go to Dimbleby Corner, Ray?'

'Well, it's just a name to me, Alison, so why not?' Rose said, smiling. 'Tell me, what is there interesting at What-you-may-call-it Corner?'

Alison gave an excited little skip.

'There's a wishing well,' she said in a hushed, mysterious voice, then broke off to throw the ball to the other end of

the lawn. Lugs tore after it. 'Well — '
the child continued, 'you say your wish,
not aloud of course, and if you are to
get it, you know, if it comes true, the
water moves. Yes, really — ' as she
caught sight of Rose's unbelieving
smile. 'It does, really.'

'The wind wouldn't be blowing,
would it?' Rose asked teasingly, and
Alison joined in her laughter. Rose
looked round the pleasant colourful
garden and spacious lawn. There were
some brightly striped garden chairs set
out under a spreading copper beech
tree. Alison skipped towards them and
Rose followed her.

'Tell me the names of the flowers,
Alison,' she suggested, pulling a chair
towards her and sitting down. 'I don't
recognise many of them. You see, the
flowers are different in a hot country
like India.'

'What kind of flowers grow there,
then?'

'Well, cannas and zinnias, and — '

'What are cannas, Ray?'

'They're a kind of — iris, I think you'd call them.'

'Good morning,' said a voice behind her, and Rose's heart gave a queer little jump.

'Mr Drake,' Alison called joyfully, and whirled round to meet the young man. 'Oh, have you come to lunch?' He laughed and looked at Rose.

'No, of course not. I'm just on my way back to the hospital, and — as I was passing here I thought I'd call in for a minute just to say good morning to you both.' He smiled at the child, then his eyes moved back to Rose's face, which had become pink and glowing all at once. 'How are you, Miss Desmond?' he asked. 'I must say you are looking very well after your journey.'

'I'm fine,' Rose said, feeling suddenly young and joyful. 'Won't you sit down?' She smiled and patted the chair next to her.

'I shouldn't really,' he said. 'But, well — just for a split second, perhaps.' His blue eyes met hers, and she blushed, a thing she had not done for years.

'What's a split second?' Alison asked, picking up the ball and throwing it again. With a bored air, Lugs lumbered after it.

Rose heard the sound of a car coming up the drive and looked across the lawn just as Alison said, 'Oh, here's Daddy.' The child's voice sounded flat, and Rose stared at her in surprise.

Robert Stanton slammed the door of the gleaming white Jaguar car, and strode across the grass towards the little group under the copper beech tree.

'Well, well,' he said, rubbing his hands together. 'And how is the new member of my family this fine morning?' He smiled at Rose and nodded casually to Laurie. His tone was jovial, but Rose got a quick impression that he was displeased at something or someone. Not at her, she was sure. Was it Laurie Drake, then? The latter got quietly to his feet with an air of vague apology; and Rose concluded that her surmise was probably correct.

'Well, I must be on my way,' he said with a quick side glance at Stanton's face. He hesitated for a moment, turned to smile at Rose and Alison; then, with a halfwave, crossed the lawn and disappeared up the drive.

Robert Stanton sat down in the chair which Laurie had vacated. He pulled it a shade nearer to Rose's and bent forward to pat her hand.

'I hope you have not been bored, Ray, my dear,' he said. 'I am a busy man; most scientists are, I am afraid. But I do have the odd afternoon free, and, of course, most evenings.'

'Daddy,' Alison said, rather timidly Rose thought, 'Ray said she would like to go to Dimbleby Corner.' The child was sitting on the grass at Rose's feet, and now she glanced up uncertainly into her father's face.

'Sure it isn't you who want to go there?' Stanton asked teasingly.

'Oh, yes, Daddy, me too, of course.' There was an over-eager air about the little girl as she watched her father's face; almost as if she were not quite sure of his temper or humour. 'May we go, then?'

'We'll see. But run in now and see if lunch is ready.'

When Alison had gone, followed by the portly Lugs, Rose turned to Robert Stanton and said, 'You mustn't let me take up too much of your time. I'm quite happy for the moment, and I suppose that after a time I shall meet people, and make friends, and get about, and — '

'Yes, of course,' he interrupted abruptly, and Rose had the impression once more that something or someone had annoyed him. His hand was still over hers, however, and now he pressed it.

'Ray,' he said, 'I am afraid you will have to make up your mind to take things quietly for a time. Till we see how you react to this climate, I mean.'

'But I feel perfectly fit,' Rose said, concealing her impatience with an effort. The steady pressure of his hand over hers was making her feel uncomfortable, and under pretext of brushing away a fly she now quietly withdrew it. 'I think it's a mistake to worry about one's ailments,' she added, feeling irritated and angry. Yet she should have known what to expect, Rose thought. Ray had told her, but, well, she hadn't really taken it seriously. Now she mentally braced herself for the first pitting of her will against his, yet knowing all the time that she must not oppose him too obviously. Surely, with all her experience of twisting men round her little finger, she could manage this one. Rose turned now and smiled meltingly into his face.

'Yes, of course I do see what you mean,' she said. 'And I will do as you advise — to begin with.'

Stanton's face cleared at once, and he stood up, drawing Rose to her feet. 'That's a good girl,' he said almost gaily. 'Come along in to lunch now; it's almost time.'

That afternoon Robert Stanton showed

Rose just how charming he could be. The three of them went out to Dimbleby Corner, Rose sitting beside Robert in the car and Alison in the back seat. All the way out he regaled her with interesting little tit-bits of history and legend to do with the towns and villages through which they passed. Rose found herself laughing delightedly at some of his anecdotes.

At the wishing well they each made a wish, and Rose saw that as Stanton made his, his eyes were fixed on her face; and for some unaccountable reason a flush rose to her cheek. Alison skipped excitedly and swore that she saw the water move. Rose laughed to hide her sudden embarrassment, and pointed out that quite a brisk breeze was blowing, anyway.

On the way back Robert asked Rose if she would like to go out to dinner that evening. She eagerly agreed, mentally reviewing Ray's wardrobe. There was the black velvet, the gold lamé, the blue-and-silver brocade — Rose thought the gold lamé. And when, a couple of hours later, Rose joined Robert Santon in the lounge, she knew by the look in his eyes that she had made a good choice.

Many admiring eyes followed Rose and her tall companion as the head waiter led them to a corner table. An excellent orchestra was playing soft seductive music, and Rose's feet began instinctively to tape out the rhythm. She wondered if Stanton was a good dancer; he looked as if he might be. The dinner and service were excellent.

'Do you dance?' Rose asked her companion during a lull in the conversation. She looked at him beguilingly over the rim of her liqueur glass.

'Yes — I do,' he said after a pause. 'But dancing is not for you, my dear Ray.' Rose looked reproachful.

'Oh, please, let me forget all that — just for tonight,' she pleaded. 'I'm so enjoying this evening — and I feel quite well.' She flashed her brilliant smile at him. 'Now do I look like an invalid?'

Stanton's eyes strayed from her

shining dark head to the bright eyes, the flower-like mouth; then down to the creamy-white of her neck and shoulders. Slowly he shook his head. 'No,' he said softly. 'You certainly do not.'

Rose knew that she was blushing under his gaze, but before she could reply he suddenly rose, took her hand and drew her to her feet.

'Come along, my dear,' he said. 'Just one,' and Rose felt a thrill of triumph run through her; she had won.

Stanton danced well, she found, and Rose enjoyed herself.

'You dance beautifully,' he told her, and as she glanced up at him with a smile upon her lips she found his eyes fixed upon her with a curiously intent look. 'You amaze and intrigue me, Ray,' he added. 'You are not the least like I expected you to be.'

'What *did* you expect?' There was a guarded note in her voice; she would have to be careful; but, after all, this man had not seen Ray since she was a child, Rose thought, and girls change a great deal from childhood to young womanhood.

'Well — ' Stanton said thoughtfully, 'judging by what I had been told in your parents' letters, I had formed a mental picture of a delicate, reserved girl; a semi-invalid, in fact, and accustomed all her life to being shielded from every worry and responsibility; in other words, just another child to care for. Whereas — '

'Yes?' Rose murmured, and looked at him from under her long lashes. She could scarcely repress a smile at the incongruity of his words. Stanton's clasp round her slender waist tightened.

'Definitely not a child,' he said in a low voice, and bent his face close to hers. 'All of a woman, my dear — and a most attractive one.'

Rose laughed lightly. She could not make up her mind as to whether she liked this man or not. He fascinated her, and she was flattered at his obvious admiration. He was handsome, wealthy, and of good standing, but —

'You are not what *I* expected, either,' she murmured provocatively.

'Tell me,' he said softly. 'In what way am *I* unexpected?'

'Well, you're younger than I thought you would be, and — ' Rose stopped. She was looking over his shoulder, and had seen a face she knew, the face of Laurie Drake, and she felt excited and happy all at once. He was sitting at a table with a party of three others, and when he caught sight of Rose his whole face seemed to light up, and he smiled and waved. Rose smiled in return, and Stanton said quickly:

'Someone you know?'

'Someone you know, too. Doctor Drake — over there,' and she nodded towards where the party were sitting. At that moment the music stopped, and Robert took Rose firmly by the arm and led her back to their table.

'What would you like to drink, my dear?' he asked, signalling to the waiter.

Rose was about to say that she would have a burra peg, but remembered just in time. Ray was probably not allowed spirits at all. Rose sighed and decided to put out a feeler.

'I'll have a gin and tonic,' she said, then added, 'If I may, of course.'

'Well — ' Stanton was beginning, when a voice came from over Rose's shoulder.

'Good evening, Miss Desmond; good evening, sir,' Laurie Drake greeted them, and Rose looked up with a welcoming smile.

'Oh, hello,' Stanton said abruptly, and turned again to the hovering waiter.

Rose turned eagerly to Laurie; she was delighted to meet up again with this very nice young man. 'Hello,' she said. 'Won't you sit down?' and she patted the chair next to her. He hesitated for a moment, glanced quickly at Stanton, then took the chair indicated. He looked again at Rose's glowing face, frank admiration in his own.

'I — I wondered if you could spare

me a dance,' he said diffidently. 'That is, if Mr Stanton — '

'Why, of course — ' Rose was beginning eagerly, when the older man cut in.

'Miss Desmond is not dancing any more tonight,' he said in firm tones and offering his cigarette-case to Rose.

'No, thank you,' she snapped, her eyes glinting with anger and resentment. This was really too much, Rose thought, then quickly she checked herself. She must remember that she was Ray, and act as *she* would have done. 'Oh, please — Mr Stanton,' she said pleadingly, and looking into his face with suddenly limpid eyes. 'Just one more, and then I promise to do everything you say.'

He hesitated, and Rose murmured softly, 'Please — I do love dancing so.'

Stanton looked into the bright eyes, then his glance strayed to the parted flower-like mouth. He glanced briefly at the other man and smiled rather frostily.

'Very well, Ray,' he said. 'But this must be definitely the last.'

Rose was hardly conscious of the music starting again, or of the fact that Laurie Drake was a very indifferent dancer. It didn't seem to matter, anyway. All Rose knew was that she felt extraordinarily happy.

'I really ought to apologise for having cheek enough to ask you to dance,' Laurie said, carefully manoeuvring Rose round a corner. 'I'm not very good, I'm afraid.'

Rose looked into his clear eyes, almost on a level with her own; and all at once she saw again the silent lake under the dawn sky. She felt again the coolness of the water sliding over her naked shoulders, and knew, suddenly, that the thing she had longed for then, and forgotten all about in the shoddy years that had followed, was near at hand if only she could see it. If only she knew what it was. Rose shrugged impatient shoulders, and smiled into the blue eyes opposite her own.

'No, you're not very good,' she agreed, a dimple appearing in one smooth cheek. 'But — I don't mind, really.'

'That's — really big of you,' the young man said gratefully. '*You* dance beautifully; it must be very frustrating not to be able to — '

'Oh, don't *you* remind me!' Rose interrupted angrily. The magic of the moment had gone with his words, and suddenly she hated the whole evening. 'Nothing is going as I thought it would,' she thought. 'Perhaps some people are right when they say that money isn't everything; *I*'ve never had the chance to find out. I wish — Oh, I wish — Oh, I don't know what I wish!'

Rose saw that Laurie was watching her eagerly. 'I'm sorry,' he said softly. 'Ray, will you come out with me one evening? Perhaps — '

Rose looked at him, and miraculously the world was right again.

'Yes, Laurie,' she said. 'I'd like to very much. When?'

5

Robert Stanton stood up as Rose and Laurie returned to the table at the conclusion of the dance. He gave a quick glance at Rose's flushed face and bright eyes and said abruptly:

'Now, my dear, it's home and bed for you. We must not over-do it, must we?' He smiled stiffly as he spoke, and pointedly ignored the other man. Laurie waited a moment, then with a smile at Rose and a word of thanks, he backed away into the crowd.

'All right; I'm ready now if you are.' Rose's voice was sharp with irritation as she turned to pick up her handbag and stole. 'Though it doesn't really matter,' she was thinking to herself. 'I shall be seeing Laurie again the day after tomorrow. He's a dear, and I quite like him.' Rose was not prepared to admit, even to herself, that she liked Laurie

Drake very much indeed. But she had noticed that, whenever she was with him, or even thought of him, those unwelcome pangs of — was it conscience? — began to niggle her. Rose resolved now to stifle them once and for all by keeping thoughts of Laurie strictly in place. He did not really enter her scheme of things. He was an attractive person; she liked his company, but that was all.

The journey home started in silence, but presently Stanton turned his head to look at Rose and said softly:

'You're not angry with me, Ray, are you?'

'No, of course not.' She would not meet his eyes, but stared straight ahead.

'I'm doing it only for your own good, my dear. Remember you are in my care now, and I am responsible for you; but presently we'll have a check-up, and really find out what that little ticker of yours is up to.' He paused, then as Rose made no reply, he added, 'Till then — be patient, Ray,' and Rose felt his hand pressing hers in her lap.

'Yes, all right,' she replied unwillingly, the back of her hand beginning to tingle. 'I will try to be patient; but truly, Mr Stanton, I feel quite well, and I hate to be pampered at every turn. Perhaps I have grown out of it. Things like that do happen.'

'Perhaps.' Stanton's hand tightened on hers, then very softly he added, 'Must it be 'Mr Stanton', Ray? Need we be so formal, especially as we shall be living together — in the same house, I mean — for years, perhaps? Why not call me Robert?'

Rose's heart seemed to miss a beat; but she managed to laugh rather breathlessly before replying, 'Yes, why not? I don't mind if you don't. 'Mr Stanton' does make you seem rather elderly, doesn't it?' With an effort she drew her hand from under his to push a lock of hair back into place, then rested it on the edge of the car door.

'Do I seem elderly to you, Ray?' His voice was quite anxious, Rose thought.

She looked sideways at him, at his handsome profile and clear-cut chin; and in spite of herself was conscious of a thrill of triumph. He was so obviously attracted to her, and was, after all, a very eligible man. But did she really like this guardian of Ray's? Rose could not make up her mind. There *was* a kind of fascination, and she was flattered at his interest in her, but was that all? She just did not know.

'No, of course not,' Rose murmured in answer to his question. 'Not a bit — elderly.'

'Would you like a little ride round before we go home?' he asked. 'It's a lovely night.' But some instinct made Rose reply quickly:

'I'd rather go straight home, if you don't mind. I *am* a little tired,' and she gave him her appealing 'little-girl' look.

'Why, of course, my dear,' he said at once, but Rose felt his shoulder press for a moment against her own.

When she got up to her room, she found the electric fire on, though the night was quite mild. The bedclothes were turned back, and Rose's nightdress was draped across the pillow. On the bedside table was a thermos flask, a cup and saucer, and a plate of biscuits. She stretched herself luxuriously, then quickly undressed and slipped into the shimmering silk nightdress. Leaning back on the pillows, Rose thought back over the events of the evening. It had been a pleasant but frustrating one, she decided, pouring herself a cup of Ovaltine from the flask. To begin with, she had not expected to see Laurie Drake again so soon; and — here Rose smiled softly to herself — he had made a date with her. He's rather sweet, she thought; he makes me feel — good. Her thoughts then turned to Robert Stanton, and a dimple showed in her cheek. It was really quite exhilarating to have two such nice, exciting men in her train. Nice in quite different ways, of course. In fact, was Robert Stanton 'nice' at all — or was he just exciting? Rose laughed silently to herself as she replaced the cup and flicked off the bedside light. It's going to be fun, anyway, she thought, and snuggled sleepily down between the soft sheets.

The next morning Rose was up, and down to breakfast, even before Alison. Robert gave her a surprised 'good morning' as he hurried in and helped himself from the hotplate. The meal was rather silent, but towards the end Stanton turned to Rose and said with a smile:

'I expect you would like to 'do' the shops, Ray, wouldn't you? Alison is going to take you out this morning, and here is something to spend,' and he dropped a cheque into her lap. Rose picked it up and saw that it was for one hundred pounds.

'Oh, but I don't want — ' she began, a sudden panic taking possession of her. But Stanton interrupted impatiently.

'Take it, my dear Ray, it's your own money. I arranged all that with the lawyers who are dealing with your affairs. We will have a business meeting soon, but in the meantime you can spend what you like, of course. Now I really must go.' He patted Alison on the head, smiled at Rose, and went quickly out of the room.

Rose picked up the slip of paper, then dropped it on the table. 'I don't want it,' she thought. 'I don't even want to touch it.' Then she stopped. What was the matter with her now? Isn't this what she had wanted when she took another girl's name? Plenty of money to spend; never again to have to worry about where the next penny was coming from? Wasn't it? Then why — ?

'Can anyone get money for cheques, Ray?' Alison's query broke in on Rose's muddled thoughts, and suddenly she picked up the cheque and put it in her handbag.

'Well, not exactly,' she said, laughing. 'The person who signs it must have an account at the bank.'

'And have you — ' the child was beginning, but Rose cut her short.

'Come on, Alison,' she said, jumping to her feet. 'I'm dying to see these shops. Let's go, shall we?'

Half an hour later, as the two girls darted excitedly from one shop to another, Rose had succeeded in stifling the unwelcome scruples of an hour or so earlier. It was a very long time since she had had so much money to spend, and so she was determined now not to spoil her own pleasure. Money and security, that's what she had wanted, wasn't it? Any complaints? No, Rose told herself defiantly, as she slipped yet another glamorous-looking frock over her head.

'Oh, Ray, that's the bestest of all,' Alison exclaimed, her eyes wide with admiration. 'Please, please, take that one.' Rose turned from side to side, glancing at herself first from one angle, then from another, then regretfully she shook her head.

'No, I've been extravagant enough for one day,' she said. 'Too extravagant really. But what about you, Alison?

Wouldn't you like something? A frock, perhaps, or a hat?'

The child stared at Rose with round eyes. 'Oh, Ray, may I really choose something?' she asked, and gave a little jump of joy. 'Oh, could I please have a swim-suit? There's a shop that sells them just up the street.'

Rose smiled down into the eager face. There was an unusual warmth stirring in her heart. Alison's a nice kid, she thought, and was suddenly glad that it was she who had brought that happy expression to the child's face; and it occurred to Rose all at once that the little girl did not always look happy, and wondered why. It could not be that she missed her mother because Rose had gathered from Mrs Branksome that the latter had been in her present situation for nearly six years. And Alison had a good home and a good father. Rose's thoughts paused here. Didn't the child seem nervous of her father sometimes? Well, perhaps not nervous, but — ill at ease; in fact, never really at her ease with him. Rose shrugged her shoulders impatiently. She was imagining things. Of course the child was all right. In any case, Alison was not *her* responsibility.

As the two girls emerged from the shop Rose almost collided with a stout man in a black-and-white checked suit. She was starting to apologise when, to her surprise, Alison stopped and said:

'Hello, Mr Sharp. How is Prince?'

'Why, hello, m'dear,' the man replied in a thick, husky voice. 'Oh, Prince? He's fine. And how's yer pa?' He was eyeing Rose as he spoke, and edging in her direction.

'Come along, Alison,' Rose said in her cool, level voice. 'We'll take a taxi home after we have been to the swim-suit shop.'

'Goodbye, Mr Sharp,' Alison called as she turned and followed Rose.

'Who was that man?' asked the latter as they continued along the street.

'Well, I don't know where he lives, Ray, but Daddy knows him. He's got some horses that ride races. At least, I think they belong to him; one is called Prince. Daddy took me one day to the races, and Mr Sharp had all the names of his horses written up on a board. Afterwards he showed me which was Prince, 'cos he won the race.'

'I see,' Rose said. So, the man was a bookie, and Robert Stanton was interested in horse-racing, was he? She would get him to take her to a meeting. It was only last year that she'd won quite a nice little pile on the Gold Cup race at Calcutta. She'd been in very low water at the time, and the money had come in handy, Rose remembered.

Alison's swim-suit was bought after much enjoyable chopping and changing of minds; and the two girls arrived home just in time for lunch. Robert listened with a slightly bored air to his daughter's account of the morning's activities, then genially suggested that they might have a run down to the coast in the afternoon. Rose caught Alison's eye and laughed.

'Just in time,' she said and pointed to the parcel which the child had left on the side table.

'Well, you both seem to have had an enjoyable morning,' Robert remarked, looking at Rose's flushed cheeks and bright eyes, and as he spoke Mrs Branksome opened the door and looked in.

'The telephone,' she said. 'For Miss Desmond.'

Rose murmured an 'Excuse me' and hurried out, after first catching sight of Robert's surprised glance. 'It will be Laurie,' she was thinking. 'Oh, I do hope — '

'Hello,' she said, picking up the receiver. 'It's Ro — Ray Desmond speaking.' She still did not find it easy to use the dead girl's name.

'Oh, hello,' came the quick reply. 'How are you? Good. Look — er — Ray, I'm terribly sorry, but I'm afraid I shall have to call off this evening's date. It's my mother, who lives in Norwich. She's ill, and I must go to her. As a matter of fact, I'm off in about ten minutes. I'm awfully sorry, Ray, and more than disappointed. Perhaps — '

'I'm sorry, too,' Rose said. 'But of course I quite understand, and I do hope you find your mother better. Please don't worry about this evening — ' she gave a little laugh. 'There are others and — '

'Yes, of course there are.' His voice sounded relieved. 'I was so looking forward to seeing you again, Ray. However — I'll give you a ring when I get back.'

'Yes, do that. Goodbye, and — I hope you will be back — soon.' Rose put down the receiver. She was more disappointed than she would care to admit, but she realised all at once how much of her happiness in the morning's shopping had depended on what was to happen in the evening. All the time she had been buying and trying on the lovely frocks and shoes, she had had Laurie and their effect upon him in mind. In fact, he was occupying quite a large share of Rose's thoughts lately. And now, she would not be seeing him again for days, perhaps weeks. She walked slowly back to the dining-room where Alison and her father were drinking coffee. A cup had been poured for her.

'What colour is your swim-suit, Ray?' Alison asked, then looked at her father. 'What time shall we start, Daddy?'

'Who was your mysterious caller, Ray?' Robert asked, ignoring the child's question; but Rose turned to her and pretended not to hear him.

'Well, I have a yellow one,' she said, 'and a black-and-white striped.'

'Oh — the yellow,' Alison said, doing her little jog, on the chair this time. 'It'll look 'fab' against my red.'

'Surely you don't swim, Ray, not with your — ' Robert began, but Rose interrupted him.

'Of course I swim,' she said, thinking of an enchanted month she had spent recently at Juhu Beach, near Bombay.

She'd had a job with a dancing troupe at the Taj Mahal Hotel that season, and had done very well for herself. A rich Parsee had fallen heavily for her, and had been kind and generous before becoming too demanding. Rose remembered even now that it had been quite a job to get rid of him. 'I'm not much of a swimmer,' she conceded. 'But — I do enjoy it,' and she gave him her quick brilliant smile.

'Well — we'll see when we get down there,' Stanton said, his pale eyes watching her vivid face.

Rose enjoyed her afternoon in spite of the restrictions placed upon her. They were down at the coast within the hour, and as the day was warm and sunny Robert Stanton allowed Rose to swim — not too far out and only for a few minutes. Rose fumed inwardly, but after a short while was quite content to laze and sunbathe on the beach while Alison splashed about in the shallows, and Stanton plunged in for some real exercise. Later on they all had tea at a beach café before returning to Farndon in the cool of the evening.

As Rose changed her dress for dinner, she thought back over the day, and the days before this. There was a sameness about it all, she thought. She stared at her face in the glass, and brushed her hair with hard, irritated strokes. The leisured classes don't really seem to get much fun out of life, Rose thought. She would not admit that her feeling of flatness was due mostly to the fact that her evening out with Laurie was off.

That evening, after Alison had gone to bed, Rose sat with Robert and watched television on the big twenty-three-inch colour screen.

'What will you have to drink, Ray?' Stanton asked, then, as she made no reply, 'What would you like to do tomorrow, my dear?'

'Oh, anything,' she said in a bored voice. The mild exhilaration of the day's outing had died down. 'This isn't what I had thought it would be; not what I'd planned or expected,' she thought. 'Well, what did I expect?' Yes, apart from having plenty of money to spend, and not having to work for a living, what had she really thought this stolen life of hers would be? The truth was, and Rose faced it now, she had not really thought at all. She had done what she had done on an impulse. And she had paddled her own canoe for so long that it just had not occurred to her that in this new life her precious liberty would be gone. She had not been able to envisage such a possibility. Unintelligent, perhaps, Rose thought now, but remembered that she had silently agreed with the dead girl when she had said, 'But, Rose dear, *you* understand men; you'd soon twist things *your* way.' Well, she knew now, didn't she? And she knew that she'd have to make a stand if what she had done was to be worth while. What was the good of having money if she couldn't please herself? *And* she was not going to wait nearly three years to do that.

'I don't know what I shall be doing tomorrow,' Rose said, eyeing Robert coolly, yet feeling slightly ashamed of her ungraciousness; he had put himself out to entertain her, after all. 'I hate everything to be planned beforehand.'

'Yes, of course, I agree, but — ' He leaned forward and patted her knee. 'You will take things easy, won't you, and not overtire yourself?'

Rose shuffled her feet impatiently. 'Why won't you let me try to forget it?' she said. 'Surely that is better than dwelling on disease, isn't it? I feel perfectly fit.' How she hated all this fussing. Rose had never had an illness in her life.

'Well — ' Stanton replied, smiling into her flushed face, 'I'm very glad to hear it. When I have five minutes to spare, I'll go through your papers again and arrange at the hospital for an examination.' Rose's heart missed a beat. She had not bargained for this. 'In the meantime, you must, I am afraid, obey doctor's orders.' He laughed teasingly and moved his chair nearer hers. 'Now, what about that drink?'

'Tell me something about your work,' Rose suggested a few minutes later as, having handed her a glass, he sat down again. He gave her a quick glance.

'D'you mean my medical research?'

'Yes,' she nodded. 'I'd love to hear about it; sounds most interesting. What are you 'researching' and where do you do it?' It will pass the evening to hear about it, she was thinking.

'Come, I'll show you,' Stanton said, rising and drawing Rose also to her feet. She followed him out of the room. He crossed the hall and drew a small key from his inside breast pocket. 'Here we are,' he said, stooping in front of a door which was screened from the rest of the hall by the wide curved staircase. 'This door is always kept locked,' he told Rose. 'It's a special lock, and the key is always in my possession.'

'Sounds just like Bluebeard's cupboard,' Rose said, laughing, as Stanton opened the door. 'I'm almost afraid to go in,' and she hung back in pretended fear.

'Nothing to be afraid of,' he said softly, slipping an arm round her waist, 'that is — if you don't touch anything.' He drew Rose forward, and she looked about her with lively curiosity. The small room looked just her idea of a chemist's laboratory, she thought. It was narrow and secretive-looking, and with only one window situated quite high up; must be rather dark during daylight hours. However, there were several clusters of electric bulbs which Stanton snapped on. It occurred suddenly to Rose that no one could snoop from outside without the aid of a tall ladder. She gave a sudden shiver, and his clasp tightened. 'Cold?' he asked.

She shook her head and moved from the circle of his arm, for she had been conscious again of the queer kind of half-attraction, half-repulsion he had for her. Rose looked at the ranks of glass-stoppered jars, bottles and tubes on the shelves. They contained liquids and powders of various colours. On a white-topped table were glass retorts and Bunsen burners. On all sides of the room were gleaming polished sinks, and on another table was an apparatus which resembled, Rose thought, an X-ray machine; and beside it were trays and trays of glass slides.

'What is this?' she asked, going up to the second table and pointing to the apparatus.

'That is to examine slides,' he replied. 'It is all to do with the experiments I am carrying out.'

'But what are the experiments — or should I not ask?' He smiled.

'You would not understand if I told you, but all these — ' he waved his hand at the rows of glass-stoppered bottles, 'contain essences of drugs — Oriental drugs.'

'And what is the research you are doing?'

'Well, generally speaking, I am trying to find out the effect of these drugs on the human organism, and then — the antidote to be used, and how to manufacture it. That's the general idea.'

Rose looked at Stanton, and saw that his strange, almost colourless eyes were alight and shining. He was not looking at her, but at the rows of bottles and jars on the shelves. This is his big interest, she thought suddenly; this is what he really loves — and gave another involuntary shiver. There was something repellent about this spotlessly-white small room.

'Are these drugs dangerous?' she asked. Stanton's eyes came back to her face with a detached kind of stare, then he laughed briefly, took Rose by the arm, and led her out of the room. He very carefully locked the door and put away the key before he answered her question.

'Dangerous!' Stanton said, and laughed again. 'My dear Ray, if, one night, I were to inject you with something from almost any one of those innocent-looking little bottles, well — it's most unlikely that you would wake up in the morning. You see, my dear — ' he smiled down into Rose's face, took her arm and led her back to the lounge, 'they are all — deadly poisons.'

6

The rest of the week passed quietly and uneventfully. Rose was becoming more and more bored as each day passed. She was accustomed to a life of hard work, constant change, and ever-recurring hazards, and — she was missing them. In fact, Rose was beginning to realise that comfort and security could also be dull and monotonous; though she had not yet reached the point where she would be willing to acknowledge at last that she was disillusioned with her present way of life. She still felt that she herself could change that way, and was now willing to bide her time.

One night there was a dinner party, followed by a visit to the theatre. Rose had looked forward to it, but was disappointed to find on the night that all the guests seemed to be married couples and verging on middle age. She enjoyed the play, but was bored by her escort, a plain, quiet man whose wife happened to be away on a visit to her mother. Rose noticed that Robert Stanton was at his most charming; skilfully and easily entertaining his guests, and at dinner keeping the ball of conversation rolling. What a queer mixture he is, she thought, watching him; and involuntarily her thoughts slipped back to the night when he had taken her to see his research laboratory. It had been interesting, of course, but queerly frightening, too. Suppose, Rose thought, suppose he lost the key one day; and someone else, someone who knew nothing at all about those deadly poisons, got hold of it; or suppose he himself — 'Stop it,' she silently ordered herself. 'You're getting soft. What are you scared of, anyway? He is a scientist engaged on research, isn't he? Well, then, put it right out of your mind, and forget about that locked-up room with the one tiny window.'

113

Rose had been giving a lot of thought lately to the problem of how to assert her own personality unobtrusively and without antagonising Robert Stanton. It was a difficult situation, as he seemed to be putting himself out to make sure that she was happy and entertained. He showered money upon her, and had twice suggested taking her to choose a car, and giving her first lessons in driving. It was all subtly tempting to Rose; but some obscure instinct which she herself could not understand and which inwardly infuriated her, made her put most of the money away in a safe place till her own plans were clear. Rose as yet had no clear idea as to what those plans would be, but she knew that she was not happy and could not go on like this much longer.

On the day after the dinner party Stanton, Rose and Alison were having tea on the lawn, the weather being still mild and sunny, when a car was heard coming up the drive.

'Oh, look, it's cousin Tim,' Alison

said excitedly, jumping to her feet, 'and his girl friend.' The car stopped and a tall, good-looking young man got out and waved to the group on the lawn. A fair-haired girl climbed out from the other side. She wore a yellow shirt with red jeans, and had an orange scarf tied round her head.

'Hello there,' the young man called as Alison raced to meet him. Rose looked at the two with eager interest. The young man, who was wearing a blue towelling shirt and white shorts, stopped to grab the child and swing her off the ground. They clowned for a moment or two, then, with one arm round Alison and the other round the waist of the blonde girl, he drew them on towards Rose and Robert.

'Hello, Uncle Robert,' he called out cheerily. 'Heard the other member of your family had arrived, so I came along to say 'How d'you do'. You remember Liz, don't you?' The fair girl smiled, then turned to look at Rose.

'Oh, hello, Tim,' Robert replied. 'Er

— yes, this is Ray, my ward. Good afternoon, Elizabeth.' His manner was not very welcoming, Rose thought, and he did not even ask the visitors to sit down. But this omission did not appear to worry the young man. He shook Rose heartily by the hand and flung himself on the grass, pulling Liz down with him. Alison sat down on his other side.

'Well, I'm very glad to meet you, Ray,' Tim Tennant said, smiling up at Rose. 'How are you liking England after — India, isn't it?' She nodded.

'I like it very much,' she said. 'Not that I have seen much of it yet.' Rose glanced at Robert's closed face, and felt sharply irritated. Why does he have to behave like this, she thought, as soon as someone younger appears? Oh, I *must* make a move soon. 'Do you live near?' she asked Tim.

'Fairly,' he replied, taking out a cigarette-case and offering it round. Rose and the fair girl each took one. 'Just the other side of London.' He flicked a lighter and held it out to the two girls in turn. 'You'll have to come and visit us soon. Not that I'm often there,' he added with a laugh. 'I work in Town, you see, and only get home for the occasional weekend, but Mum would love to have you. Perhaps Uncle Robert — ' There was an almost imperceptible pause before the older man nodded and murmured something.

'But how nice of you to come and welcome me,' Rose said. She glanced again at Stanton's stiff face, hesitated for a moment, then said in a clear voice, 'You'll have some tea, won't you? Alison dear, run and tell Mrs Branksome to bring fresh tea and sandwiches, and — pull up a couple more chairs before you go.'

'No, no, please don't bother,' Tim said quickly. 'We've had tea, and can only stay a moment.' He smiled up at her. 'But look here, Ray, how about making a 'four' with us this evening? There's a jolly little road-house we

117

know. We could call for you about seven. How about it?'

Before Rose could reply, Robert quickly intervened. 'I'm afraid not, Tim,' he said. 'Ray is leading a very quiet life — for the moment, at any rate. She is not at all strong, and dancing is quite out of the question.'

The young man looked surprised and rather embarrassed.

'Sorry, sir,' he said. 'I'm afraid I'd forgotten about — well, er — ' He got to his feet. 'Perhaps another time,' he said to Rose, whose face had flushed crimson. 'A 'flick', perhaps. I'll give you a ring sometime. Anyway, we can show you a bit of the country, very restful and all that. You're staying here, of course?'

'For the moment,' Rose said rather loudly, and not looking at Stanton. 'Yes, do give me a ring — and soon. I'd love to make up a 'four'.'

'That's fine,' Time replied heartily. 'Come on, Liz.' He pulled his companion to her feet, then smiled again at

118

Rose who had also risen. 'Get better soon. Cheerio, Uncle Robert.'

Alison went skipping along beside the two as they made their way to the car, and on an impulse Rose followed her. She was furious with Stanton and had kept quiet only with a great effort. But the incident had made her even more determined to assert herself once and for all. It was quite obvious to Rose that if it rested with Robert Stanton she would be tied hand and foot. It also seemed obvious that he did not want her to form friendships with other young people, particularly young men.

Tim had waited when he saw that Rose was following them.

'I say, what a bore not being able to dance,' he said to her. 'What do you do with yourself all day — and night?'

'Awful bore,' echoed his companion. 'Why, life's hardly — ' Then she stopped and gave an embarrassed laugh.

'Life's hardly worth living,' that's what she was going to say, Rose thought, and was inclined to agree with her.

'Well, well,' Tim cut in hastily. 'Cheerio, chaps. Pile in, Liz. Bye-bye, Alison. 'Bye, Ray.' And with a skirl and a skid of tyres they were off. Tim did not repeat his invitation, Rose thought bleakly as she turned slowly away; no, they don't want to be hampered by crocks — and I don't blame them. Alison linked her arm in hers, and the two turned back to where Robert was still sitting.

'I didn't know you had relatives living so near,' Rose remarked. 'You have never — '

'Tim is not a relative,' Stanton broke in shortly. 'His mother and my late wife were old friends. The 'uncle' and 'cousin' business grew up with the years. No, as a matter of fact, I have no relations at all.'

'Liz has been Tim's girl friend for a long time, hasn't she, Daddy?' Alison began, but he interrupted her impatiently and said:

'Isn't it time you took that dog for his run?' The child turned at once and Rose said quickly:

'I'll come with you, Alison.' Robert's face darkened as he looked at Rose.

'I have something to say to you,' he said sharply.

'It can wait,' she replied, and went off beside Alison.

Then Rose saw that the child was looking nervous.

'Daddy's angry,' she said. 'Please don't make him angry, Ray.' Rose looked down at the small flushed face. Was it possible that Stanton might take it out on the child? She hadn't thought of that. Rose put an arm round Alison's shoulders and gave her a comforting squeeze.

'O.K., kid,' she said, and turned and went back to Stanton. 'What — was it you wanted to say?' she asked, and sat down beside him. Stanton was silent for a moment as he studied Rose's flushed and mutinous face. His own was still hard and closed.

'You make things very difficult, Ray,' he said at last. 'You know as well as I do that a quiet life is the only one for you, and I, as your guardian, must see that you do live quietly. I must say that I am surprised, and puzzled, by your attitude, Ray. You seem to resent these necessary restrictions; yet surely you must be accustomed to them by now. You have been sheltered and guarded from undue exertion all your life; at least, that was what I understood from your father's letters. Yet you behave as if all these restrictions have only recently started, since you have been here, in fact. It is something which I cannot understand, and I find it very worrying. Are you not happy here, Ray?' Rose was silent for a moment as she stared straight in front of her. Of course, it was quite true what he said. Yet why should he be so concerned? What was it to him, even if she were the real Ray? Robert Stanton was an attractive man, and certainly a personality, but Rose had never felt that he was a kind man, or the sort who would be unduly concerned about the welfare of others, even the daughter of an old friend like, presumably, Ray's father. Was it that he was getting fond of his ward, and wanted to fend off other men? Was that the explanation, and was it a welcome one to her? Rose saw that he was watching her face with a curiously intent look on his own.

'I'm sorry, Robert,' she said abruptly. 'It's true what you say, of course, but — it does seem as if you want to keep me behind a sort of screen, and I'm certainly not used to that, anyway. Oh, I know that you mean well, but don't you see that — it can't go on for ever like this? I — '

'My dear,' Robert interrupted gently, and laid his hand on hers. 'I know it must seem irksome to you, but, well — I have become very fond of you, Ray, and it worries me when you want to take unnecessary risks. Perhaps I rather overdid it, but, I *want* to look after you, my dear.' He bent his head to hers and

Rose looked up suddenly into those almost colourless eyes of his. It was as if he had willed her to do it, yet she shrank away with a queer little breathless feeling. She was attracted and repelled at the same time. Could it be that he is in love with me, she wondered, and if so, what then? Her heart began to beat unevenly as Stanton's face bent nearer; but, with a stiff little jerk backwards, Rose twisted sideways and got to her feet. With a conscious effort she dragged her gaze away from his face and mumbled:

'Yes, all right, I'm sorry, Robert.' Rose had a panicky desire to run from him, but she could not have said why. He sounded kind and solicitous for her well-being, *and* he said he was fond of her, so why could she not believe in him? But a sixth sense warned Rose to be careful. 'I'm sorry,' she said again, and edging away from him. 'It's getting rather chilly, don't you think? I — I think I'll go in.' He nodded, but did not get up.

At the door Rose was met by Mrs Branksome, who was on her way out. 'Oh, Miss Desmond,' she said. 'Telephone call for you.'

Rose's heart jumped a beat. She drew a deep, shuddering breath as if just coming awake. With a rush of excited relief, she thought, 'Laurie, it must be Laurie. Oh, I do hope it is.' Her heart was still doing queer things as she picked up the receiver with slightly unsteady fingers.

'Hello — Ray?' Yes, it was *his* voice. 'Laurie Drake here. I've just got back; well, a couple of hours ago to be exact. Oh, I'm fine. How are you? Good.' There was a pause, and Rose waited.

'How is — ' she was beginning, just as he started again.

'Ray, when may I — oh, please go on.'

'How is your mother?' Rose asked rather breathlessly.

'Very much better, thanks. In fact, she's out of the wood now, and my married sister is with her till she is on her feet again. Er — look, Ray, is there any chance of seeing you soon — this evening, perhaps?' Bright colour flooded Rose's cheeks. She felt as shy and excited as a schoolgirl, and forgot to be amused by it.

'Yes, yes, of course there is,' she said, her words almost tumbling over each other. 'I'd — I'd love to see you, Laurie.' All at once the world was a different place; everything in it was new and thrilling. Even Robert Stanton had changed from a vaguely sinister figure into a kind, though perhaps over-fussy guardian and protector. And at the thought of Robert, Rose came down to earth with a jolt of dismay. This evening! What would he have to say to this date? Would he forbid her to go? No, Rose decided, that must not happen on any account. She must get round him, somehow. Laurie was speaking again. What about a cinema, he was saying. Yes, that's it, Rose thought. Robert couldn't possibly object to that; no exertion there — or could he?

'Yes, Laurie, I'd love it,' she said. 'That'll suit me fine. What? You'll be here at seven, then? Lovely. Well — goodbye for now.'

Rose put down the receiver, and watched Robert cross the lawn and come in at the front door. She smiled at him sweetly and joined him as he went towards the library. His face was still set and glum.

'Robert,' Rose said coaxingly, 'I'm sorry if I sounded rude and ungrateful just now. I do see now that I was unreasonable.' He looked down at her in some surprise, and Rose slid her arm through his. 'It will have to be a quiet life for me — just as it always has been, I can see that.' She looked up at him appealingly, and he squeezed the arm against his side.

'That's a sensible girl,' Stanton said, looking relieved. 'I knew you would come to my way of thinking, my dear. I know it must seem rather dull for you, and I wish I could take you out in the evenings more often, but — '

'An evening at the cinema would be all right, wouldn't it, Robert?' Rose asked him innocently.

'Oh yes, that could not do you any harm.' He paused for a moment, then added, 'We must do that one evening, eh?'

'Oh, that would be marvellous.' She smiled up at him again. 'Then — it would be all right for me to go this evening?' He turned and looked at her in puzzled surprise. Rose continued. 'You see, Doctor Drake has just telephoned to ask if I would care to go with him — this evening. It's a good film, and I'd like so much to see it. You wouldn't mind, would you?' She looked at him appealingly, and saw the baffled look on his face. He hesitated, obviously trying to think of something to say against it, then replied very reluctantly:

'No — of course not. That would be all right.' His tone was grudging. 'But remember, Ray, no dancing afterwards. Straight home to bed, you know.'

'Of course,' Rose agreed, her lips compressed into a thin line. 'This is ridiculous,' she was thinking. 'One would imagine I was a sickly child.' Then, with a thrill of triumph, Rose thought, 'I've got my way with him this time.'

Laurie came along sharp at seven. Rose was wearing a black velvet frock and over it a multi-coloured brocade stole. Her dark eyes shone, and in spite of her ivory cheeks without a trace of colour, her whole face seemed to glow and pulse with life. She was having cocktails with Robert when Laurie was shown in. He greeted Robert in his usual quiet, rather diffident fashion, then turned to Rose.

'Are you — ?' he began, but Stanton interrupted him.

'Have a drink, my dear chap,' he said.

'Well — er — thanks, but — ' Laurie hesitated, but the older man added impatiently:

'Come on, man, you have plenty of time. Now, what's it to be? Ray, another one for you, my dear, same again?'

'Oh, no you don't,' thought Rose. 'You're going to try and keep us here till it's too late for the cinema, aren't you? But you won't.'

'No, thank you, Robert,' she said briskly. 'We haven't the time, and I'd hate to miss the beginning of the programme. Besides, we're having dinner first.' She put down her glass and rose to her feet.

'Why not have dinner here?' Stanton suggested in his most charming voice. 'I expect it's ready.' He turned to the rather embarrassed Laurie. 'Sit down.' The young man began to look harassed, but quietly stood his ground.

'No, it's not ready,' Rose said, picking up her handbag. 'Also I told Mrs Branksome there would be only two for dinner tonight — so there certainly won't be enough for four; and in any case, it won't be ready till the usual time — seven-thirty.' She turned to look at Laurie who now took a quick step towards the door. Robert looked at

Rose and laughed suddenly.

'You think of everything, my dear, don't you?' he said.

'I try to.' She smiled sweetly at him, then turned to Laurie. 'Ready?' she asked him, and he nodded smilingly.

'Quite ready,' he said, and a sudden faint colour stained Rose's cheeks as she caught the look of admiration in his eyes. Stanton said nothig, but watched first one young face, then the other. His eyes narrowed.

'Look after her, won't you?' he said to Laurie, his eyes watching Rose's tell-tale face. 'You know about her — disability, I think?' She glanced at him quickly. 'And so, as a doctor, I can trust her with you. But apart from all that — ' He moved suddenly and swiftly to Rose's side and slid an arm round her shoulders, smiling down into her set face as he did so. She stood stiffly within his embrace, and he squeezed her to him tenderly. 'Apart from that — ' he repeated, and looked across at the other man, 'she is rather precious to me, anyway. Good night, my dear, look after yourself. Straight home later, remember.' He turned her reluctant face to his, and kissed Rose on the cheek — then laughed softly.

'Mr Stanton has grown very fond of you, Ray,' Laurie remarked as he held the car door open for her to get in. 'But he need not worry about *me* not looking after you.' Rose gave him a quick side glance as she settled herself beside him. Yes, he really means it, she thought; he's the kind of person who never thinks wrong of anyone; he doesn't see double meanings. And at once that uncomfortable something inside her awoke and began to ask the same old questions. But again Rose turned from it angrily, and refused to search for the answers. 'Where would you like to go for dinner?' she heard Laurie say.

'May I leave it to you?' Rose replied, wondering all at once why she liked this very ordinary young man so much. He was nothing special to look at, she decided, as well as being quiet and rather shy in manner. In fact, quite the opposite to Robert Stanton. Yet it was Laurie Drake to whom she was drawn and not Robert Stanton. Laurie gave Rose a sense of peace and awareness to things of which she had taken little account up to now. I suppose it has to do with values, she thought; and yet, what has he ever said or done to make me feel that he is different? Nothing, really; and, I suppose, he's penniless, too. Watch your step, Rose told herself, this is *not* what you had in mind. But then another sly little thought edged its way in. Money didn't really matter — to her. She had plenty, and would have complete command of it if and when she married. This sudden idea excited Rose, and yet she could not quite believe in it.

'We'll go to the 'Miramar',' Laurie said. 'It's nice and handy to the cinema, and the food there is excellent. I'm awfully glad you were able to come, Ray.' Rose met the glance of his clear, candid eyes, and flashed at him her quick brilliant smile. He blinked.

'So am I,' she said, and there was a friendly silence between them till Laurie drew up outside the restaurant.

'Tell me what you have been doing lately,' he asked a few minutes later as they settled themselves at a table. He passed the menu to her. 'Though I suppose you are not able to — '

'Look,' Rose interrupted, putting the card down and looking straight at him. 'I want you to promise me something, will you?' He smiled in surprise at her intent face.

'Why, of course, if I possibly can,' he replied.

'Well, will you promise never to mention my — health, please? In fact, forget it — as I have. I'm not nearly as delicate as my guardian seems to think. I feel *fine*, so for heaven's sake let me go on feeling that way.' Laurie leaned across the table and put his hand over hers.

'I'll do that, Ray,' he said gently. 'And

I'll never speak of it again.' Rose smiled into his face. He was as easy to read as a book, and she knew that he did not believe her. 'You are a wise girl,' Laurie added. 'The mind, and what we believe, has an extraordinary effect on the body. In fact, we are only just beginning to find out exactly how much. It's a very fascinating subject.'

'Yes, I guess it is,' Rose agreed, never having given a single thought to the effect of her mind on her body. She knew the latter was in perfect condition, and up to now the workings of her mind had never given her cause for thought. She glanced across at Laurie and turned her hand so that her palm rested against his; and saw the blood creep into his fresh cheeks. 'I missed you,' Rose said.

'I — I missed you, too.' He looked deep into her dark, brilliant eyes. 'I'd almost forgotten how lovely you are. Tell me, Ray, are you happy living at 'The Gables'? What do you do all day?'

'Oh — it's all right,' Rose said with

an air of indifference. 'We go out in the car quite a lot; Robert's going to teach me to drive and soon I shall have my own car. The other night there was a dinner party — not much fun, really. All middle-aged folk, stuffy and dull. Alison's a nice kid. We go out together quite a lot, but she starts school on Monday.' The waiter arrived at that moment, and Laurie quickly withdrew his hand. He gave the order, and after the man had gone, turned again to Rose.

'Are you making a permanent home with the Stantons?' he asked, watching Rose's face.

'Well, I don't know,' she said, after a moment's hesitation, then, slowly, 'I don't really want to, it's so quiet, and rather — boring. In fact, there's nothing for me to do.'

'No, I suppose not,' he agreed. 'Though I expect you will find things to do as time goes on, and — er — you must be accustomed to a secluded life. What did you do in your home in

India? But then — ' He smiled. 'You must have had even less to do out there, with dozens of servants to wait on you, or am I out-of-date, and are things different since the partition of India?'

'Yes, everything is different,' Rose replied, and was glad that the waiter arrived at that moment. She did not want to discuss her life in India with Laurie. In fact, she could not, without lying. Though why that should worry me I really don't know, Rose thought bleakly. So, as soon as the man had gone again, she quickly changed this uncomfortable subject.

'Have you seen Mr Stanton's research lab?' she asked. 'He showed it to me one evening; it's quite fascinating — in a way.' Laurie looked at her in some surprise.

'You have been honoured,' he said. 'That's his 'Holy of Holies'. Scarcely anyone has been in there; and no one really knows what exactly is going on.' Rose told him what Robert had said to her, and he listened intently, then nodded.

'Yes, he's been at work on those lines for years, I believe, though no one ever hears of any results of the experiments; but then, scientific research is like that. He keeps it all very dark.' But Rose was getting rather tired of this impersonal topic.

'We'll have to hurry,' she reminded him, 'or we'll miss the beginning of the big feature.'

Ten minutes later they were seated side by side in the dark cinema, and to Rose's pleased surprise, Laurie had felt for her hand, and was holding it in a warm, firm clasp. She had not expected this boyish gesture, and yet it fitted him, she thought. His simplicity, his quiet directness and honesty; and again something stirred in her heart; something that was making her feel more and more uncomfortable; almost unhappy. And Rose found herself wishing suddenly that she was different; and then was angry with *him* for causing her to feel like this. So much so that abruptly she withdrew her hand from his. 'Why does he have this effect on me?' Rose thought. 'I'm not bad. I've never been knowingly unkind to anyone in my life, and, in spite of everything, I've kept men in their place; and I'm still, strange as it may seem — a virgin. I've used men, that's all, and why not when the fools were so willing to be used? You are a cheat,' the voice suddenly said. 'You take all and give nothing. You're even doing it with Robert Stanton, or trying to. But watch your step; you're not as clever as you think.'

'Did you enjoy it, Ray?' Laurie asked, turning to her as the lights went up. Rose saw that he was watching her face anxiously. 'Do you feel all right?' A spurt of anger made Rose's eyes flash.

'I told you — ' she was beginning, then stopped. It was not his fault. He was a doctor and, of course, he could not dismiss it completely from his mind. 'Yes, I'm fine,' she said shortly.

The evening was not going as Rose had hoped.

Laurie was quiet on the way home, and Rose knew that he had noticed the withdrawal of her hand in the cinema. But on arrival, and before opening the car door, he turned to her, leaned over and gently kissed her on the lips.

'Good night, Ray,' he said. 'I'll be ringing you again — quite soon, if I may.' He waited.

'Yes, of course you may,' Rose said, breathing a little faster than usual. 'I've loved this evening, Laurie — really I have. I — shall look forward to hearing from you. Good night.'

'What a man of surprises,' she thought, as very quietly she went straight up to her room. 'Somehow — I didn't expect him to kiss me.' She smiled to herself. 'But, having done so, I didn't expect him to stop at one. Oh, well, I suppose I just don't understand his sort.'

The next day and the next passed quietly for Rose. She saw Robert only in the evening and at meals, and he was always pleasant and charming to her. He had not asked her how she had enjoyed the evening at the cinema. Then, on the third evening, as they sat over glasses of sherry before dinner, he asked Rose if she would like to go out to dinner the following evening, and suggested making up a 'foursome'. Rose looked at him, at his handsome face and tall, distinguished figure, and wondered at her own feelings, or rather lack of them. Yet the telephone had only to ring and she would find herself listening breathlessly to hear if the call were for her.

'How about it, Ray?' Stanton asked again. 'Would you like that?' He rose and crossed to the couch on which she was sitting. Rose moved uneasily as he sat down beside her and took her hand in his.

'Ray, my dear,' he said softly, 'I know we have not known each other very long, and perhaps I ought not to say this so soon, but I have become very fond of you. Perhaps you guessed that, did you?' Rose tried to draw her hand away, but he kept it firmly in his. 'Yes, I expect you can guess what I am going to say.' She turned her head sharply away as he bent suddenly towards her. 'Ray,' he murmured again, 'I realise that I'm a lot older than you, dear, but I think, I hope, that I could make you happy. There is nothing I want more than to care for you for the rest of your life. Will you marry me, Ray?'

Rose's heart was beating now with great painful thuds. Every nerve in her body strained away from Robert Stanton. She could feel his fascination reaching out to her, but it filled her now with a kind of repulsion. Why, she did not know. She did not love him; but that was no reason for her to feel this horrified distaste. He was merely asking her to marry him; making an honourable proposal of marriage; yet it filled Rose with more repugnance than some of the more dubious proposals she had had in the past. She had been able to laugh at those, but this — His arm was now creeping round her shoulders, and she could not move further back away from him.

'Well, Ray?' he whispered.

'I'm sorry,' Rose muttered. 'I really am sorry, Robert, but — '

'No, don't answer now,' Stanton said quickly. 'I understand. You'd like to think it over, of course. It's a big step to take, I know. Yes, think it over for a few days, Ray, then — ' But Rose had already made up her mind. She must end this once and for all.

'I'm sorry,' she said again, but in a decisive voice. 'Thank you for asking me, and I do appreciate it, but, no, Robert, definitely no. I — I don't care for you in that way, and — I never could. You — have been very kind, but I couldn't marry you, Robert.' There was a short, almost electrical silence, then Stanton removed his arm and drew back.

'Very well,' he said in a carefully-controlled voice. 'I won't pretend that this is not a big disappointment, Ray. I had thought — but perhaps I have rushed matters, is that it?' Rose shook her head.

'No,' she said. 'It isn't that. I — just couldn't, that's all. I'm sorry you said it. I — I don't want to marry. Please don't — '

'Ray,' he interrupted, 'if it is your health you are worried about; that it is perhaps not wise for you to think of marriage, well — ' But she broke in again, a hint of panic in her voice:

'No, it's nothing like that. My — health has nothing to do with it. Please, Robert, let's leave it at that. I am grateful to you for asking me, but — no.'

Rose looked into his face just a second before he turned his head away, and was suddenly afraid of what she saw in those queer, colourless eyes of his. There was anger, and also a kind of implacable resolve in them. She shrank away from him, and wondered how she could ever have thought him attractive.

There was a minute's silence, then Stanton rose, and spoke in his usual pleasant tone of voice.

'Very well, Ray, my dear, if that is your last word. Just forget what I said, and everything shall be as it was before. How about another drink?'

Rose was glad when the long evening ended and she was able to say good night and go to her room. She felt exhausted both physically and mentally. She knew that she had come to the cross-roads, but was too tired to even attempt to solve her problems. The situation here had become impossible, but she pushed all thoughts from her, and dropped eventually into an uneasy sleep. Rose's last coherent thought was, 'I'll do something about it tomorrow. I must.'

It was in the small hours of the morning that she awoke completely, and sat up in bed. For a long time Rose sat there quite motionless and staring into the blackness in front of her. All her past life seemed to rise up before her. All the shabby and mean things she had done; and then the last one of all. The big deception. Rose faced it all at last, and stopped making excuses for herself. 'Of course it was wrong,' she whispered soundlessly into the darkness. 'Wrong and wicked. Even though I didn't cheat Ray, and it was only what she herself suggested. It was wrong, wrong just the same. I'm living a lie. My whole life now is a lie. There is nothing real about me any longer. I wasn't much before, but I was a real person. Now, I'm just a shabby, empty sham. How can Laurie *like* me?' And at the thought of him Rose clenched her hands till the nails bit into the palms.

'I'm in love with him,' she whispered. 'But it is hopeless. He doesn't know me. If he did — He doesn't even know my real name, and I can never, never tell him.' She suddenly threw herself across the pillows, and burst into a storm of weeping. 'What am I to do, what *can* I do?' Her hopeless thoughts ran on and on as she clutched the pillow to her mouth. 'Oh, God, I'm caught; and it's all my own doing — a trap I set for myself,' Rose's thoughts flashed back to the ship, to the night of Ray's death. 'Oh, what a stupid fool I was; what a fool to imagine for one moment that such a plan was workable. But it could have been,' that inner voice seemed to say. 'It's that something inside you, that something that won't give you any peace. Your conscience, perhaps. You didn't know you had one, did you? No,' Rose thought and became quiet all at once. 'It is Laurie, with his simple goodness and honesty. He makes *me* feel cheap and nasty.' She raised herself again and sat with her arms round her knees. 'I'm sick of my life,' she suddenly thought, 'I'm tired of being — nothing. I want to be a *real* decent person, for the first time in my life. What shall I do?'

Rose looked like a woe-begone child, with the tears hanging on her long black lashes and trickling down her cheeks. 'You know what to do,' the something inside her said. 'You must get clear of it all. This money is not yours; this life is not yours. START BEING YOURSELF AGAIN.' She caught her breath and stared into the blackness. But how? And at once came the reply: 'Tell the truth, pay back what you have spent, somehow; and start again. Stand on your own feet.' Well, she had done that for most of her life, Rose thought, staring into nothingness, and she supposed she could do it again. But to tell what she had done! That was something else, something quite terrifying. Could they put her in prison? And then, for the first time, another thought seemed to crash into her mind. To whom did the money belong — after Ray? Who?

Strangely enough, Rose had never given a thought to this, and her heart began to pound with a vague feeling of foreboding. 'I must find out somehow,' she thought now. After Ray — but she'd assumed, without really thinking about it at all, that Ray would have married

148

— and had children — just as she herself — and the money would have passed on, but — there must be something in the will about that. What was the phrase? Something like 'in the event of there being no issue' — well, what then? Oh, what does it matter? It's not yours. 'God! I'm so tired.' She shook her head wearily from side to side. 'But it's no use. I'll have to clear up this mess I am in. I can't go on like this any longer.'

Quite suddenly she fell into an exhausted sleep, and when she at last opened her eyes again it was to the sound of the morning tea-tray being placed beside her on the table. The sun was shining in at the window and a cool flower-scented breeze blew in. The events of the previous evening, and her subsequent reactions in the small hours of the morning, seemed to Rose now more like a nightmare than a reality. Then, as thoughts began to crowd her mind again she shrank from them in anger and frustration. 'Oh, don't be a soft fool,' Rose told herself. 'It's too late to change things now. You can't back out now, it's *too late*. And stop *worrying* about things.' Then, as her thoughts passed on to Robert Stanton, Rose got out of bed and wandered restlessly to the window. Idly and almost unseeingly, she watched Lugs sniffing at a spot on the lawn; he was missing Alison, of course. 'I can't stay here,' Rose suddenly thought. 'And yet, if I leave Farndon, I leave Laurie, and — I love him. But — ' She turned away from the window in despair. 'It's hopeless, anyway. I could never tell him the truth about me, he'd never understand. He'd be shocked and horrified; he might even consider it his duty to go to the police.

'Well,' the voice inside her said, but it was very faint this time, 'wouldn't *anything* be better than this web of lies in which you are living, and will be living FOR THE REST OF YOUR LIFE?'

'Oh, God, no,' Rose said, and realised that she had spoken aloud, 'No, no,

150

anything but that.' She sat down by the dressing-table, and a quietness came over her; and she knew that in that moment her decision had been made. Whatever the cost, she must get free of all this and become a real person again. She flinched and almost fainted at what she knew she must do, and what might happen as a result. 'But it's got to be done,' Rose thought, 'and — I'm pretty tough, anyway.' She set her teeth and tried to be calm about it all. 'I've done a dreadful thing, but I'm going to try to put it right. If it means losing Laurie, well' — she shrugged weary shoulders — 'it's just too bad.'

At breakfast Robert Stanton was his usual charming self; so much so that Rose began to wonder if she had imagined that look in his eyes when she had refused his proposal; that coldly implacable look.

'Well, Ray, and what are you going to do with yourself this morning?' he asked, watching her face as she poured a cup of coffee. 'You must be missing

Alison since school started again.'

'I am,' Rose replied, not looking at him. An idea had come into her mind. 'I might have a look round the shops; there's a record I want to order.'

'We might go out in the car this afternoon, if you like,' Robert casually suggested. 'What about those driving lessons? And have you thought any more about the car?' Rose shook her head, then glanced sideways at him and wondered again if she had been mistaken. Surely it was natural for him to have shown annoyance at having been turned down. But was that all?

'Yes, all right,' she murmured. 'I'd like to go out this afternoon.' He picked up the morning paper, made a few comments on the news of the day, then excused himself and hurried out of the room. Rose waited till she had seen the car disappear up the drive, then, putting on a light coat and picking up her handbag, she also went out.

At the corner of the road she picked up a bus which took her into the centre of the town. But instead of turning in the direction of the shops, she went into a telephone box, found the number of Messrs Cox and Flinders, solicitors dealing with the affairs of Miss Ray Desmond, and asked for an appointment. A pleasant, friendly voice invited Rose to come along right away if that were convenient.

Rose found the offices without much trouble, and was taken at once into the presence of Mr Cox, the senior partner. After a few polite preliminaries, Mr Cox said, looking over the rims of his spectacles:

'Well now, what can we do for you, Miss Desmond? Your guardian has no doubt told you all the details of your late father's will, but we shall be very pleased to supply any further information you may require.' He smiled at Rose paternally.

'Well — er — ' she began, then stopped. This was not going to be easy. It may well be that she should know the answers to the questions she wished to ask. Mr Cox evidently thought so. But why had Robert never mentioned it? Probably because he also thought she knew everything that was necessary — and he was a busy man, of course. Rose remembered now that he *had* spoken once of having a business talk soon. He's probably forgotten, she thought now, especially if everything *is* cut and dried and in order. Rose herself had never gone beyond looking forward to a long life of ease with marriage, husband and children as a matter of course — till last night. 'I must have been stark, staring mad,' she thought, and still did not realise that it was the change in herself that had brought about this situation. She saw that Mr Cox was watching her in some surprise.

'Can I help you in any way?' he asked. 'Are you worried about something to do with the will?' Rose shook her head.

'No, oh no,' she murmured hastily. 'It's just that — Mr Cox, you know, I suppose — about my state of health, and that I have to be very careful, otherwise — ' She hesitated, then looked away.

'Yes, yes, my dear young lady, your guardian has told me something of this, and — believe me, I am very, very sorry. I hope most sincerely that things will improve for you.' He smiled brightly at Rose. 'While there's life there's hope, you know, especially when one is young.'

'Yes, I know,' Rose agreed. 'It's just that — well, suppose something did happen, quite suddenly, as it might well do with my sort of heart — ' Mr Cox looked his sympathy, and Rose felt sick and ashamed of all the lies she was telling, but — she had to find out. 'It's about the money,' she blurted out at last. 'I — wondered if I ought to make a will of my own.' It was all Rose could think of saying, and she was prepared for the surprise on the face of Mr Cox.

'Oh, but that would be quite unnecessary,' he said. 'Perhaps it was not made quite clear to you, Miss

Desmond, but what it means is that you have a life interest in the estate, and — '
Here he smiled at Rose paternally. 'If you don't mind me saying so, my dear, you look as if a long and happy life is before you. In any case, you will almost certainly marry, and have a family, I hope so. Your children will be your heirs, and — '

'But — but — ' Rose's voice was curiously breathless as she asked her question. 'Suppose I never marry or have children?'

'Then, in that case — ' Mr Cox looked in mild surprise at her flushed face and over-bright eyes, 'according to your late father's will, the next beneficiary is ROBERT STANTON, and *his* heirs.'

8

Rose walked away from the offices of Cox and Flinders and turned almost blindly in the direction of the bus stop; but half-way there she changed her mind. She decided to go into a café, have a coffee and think things out. Mr Cox's disclosure had not yet made its full impact on her mind. Rose was afraid to face it; afraid of the fear and bewilderment that could descend upon her. She sat down at an empty table and ordered her coffee. Now, don't be a fool, and don't panic, she told herself. You are living among civilised, conventional people in the twentieth century. Why should this news come as such a shock? And then before her mind's eye she seemed to see Robert Stanton's face, and the look in his eyes when she had refused to marry him. Cold and implacable they had been. Implacable?

Rose thought, but that's ridiculous. After all, he can't marry me against my will. The waitress brought the coffee and Rose poured herself a cup. But — he wants the money — that's all, really. Perhaps he is in debt over his research work, and thought it was an easy way out. That laboratory, that is his real love, not you, or any woman. Well, then — but Rose's thoughts came to a full stop here, for what was in her mind was too fantastic — and horrifying — for words.

She remembered all at once that she was to go out with Stanton this very afternoon. 'No, I can't,' Rose thought, her breath catching in her throat. 'But — I must, I mustn't let him think that I — ' She arrived back just in time for lunch. Robert was just taking his place.

'Had a nice morning?' he enquired. 'What did you buy?' His manner was so easy and pleasant that Rose had a sudden reaction. What was the matter with her, she thought, behaving like a hysterical fool in imagining all kinds of ridiculous things; in fact, she felt heartily ashamed of her doubts and misgivings. After all, what was there so strange about Robert having asked her to marry him? She was attractive, Rose knew that very well; and he was an attractive man — well, most women would consider him so. She herself had thought so till she realised that she was in love with Laurie.

'Yes, it was quite a pleasant morning,' Rose replied. 'I shop-gazed and then had a coffee at 'Morny's' — quite nice.'

'Ready for a pleasant afternoon, too?' he asked, smiling, then added, 'Where would you like to go?' They discussed the merits of various places and, having decided, passed easily on to other topics. 'What a fanciful fool I have been,' Rose thought. 'Forget it.'

The afternoon was a complete success. Robert drove them down to the coast, stopping for tea on the way. He was at his most charming, and completely ignored the events of the previous day. In fact, he treated Rose just as any older man would treat a young girl whom he was taking for an afternoon's jaunt. On the way back he brought up once more the subject of driving lessons, and then went on to discuss the make of car best suited to a beginner. In view of her overnight decision, it all seemed half-dream, half-nightmare to Rose. She had not even started to make her own plans. The future loomed desolately before her.

It was still early evening when they arrived back home, and as Rose walked into the hall she heard the shrill ring of the telephone. Her pulse quickened. Would it be for her? It was not a time when Robert often had calls. Almost at the same moment Mrs Branksome called out:

'For you, Miss Desmond, telephone.' Rose's heart leapt. It would be Laurie; it must be.

'Hello, Ray.' How dear his voice had become. 'I've got an unexpectedly free evening. What about you? Could you meet me for dinner? You could? Good-o, that's fine. Shall I call for you, or — ' There was a note of hesitation in his voice, and Rose replied at once:

'No, Laurie, I'll meet you at the 'Miromar'. What time?'

'Well — ' His voice was apologetic. 'I have to be back by ten, unfortunately, and I'm not *quite* sure when I shall be off — ' He paused again. 'I've got an awful cheek asking you at all, but — well, I did want to see you again, Ray, and it's not always easy to — ' But Rose cut him short.

'Don't apologise,' she said softly. 'I want to see you, too. We can have a couple of hours, anyway. I'll be there at about — ' she glanced down at her watch, 'eight. And if you are not there, I'll wait in the lounge. How's that?'

Rose replaced the receiver quietly on its stand. She had just heard Stanton come in. Noiselessly she started up the stairs.

'Ray,' he called. 'Come and have a drink before you go up to change.' He was standing at the door of the lounge now and was watching her. Rose came slowly down again.

'I won't be in to dinner,' she said. 'I'm having dinner with Laurie Drake.' There was silence as she walked into the room, followed by Stanton.

'Will you have sherry or a cocktail?' he asked. 'Sit down, my dear, and I am afraid I must ask you not to go out again. You have been out enough for one day, and I think a quiet evening and early to bed is indicated.' Rose looked at his face half bent over the drinks cabinet, and her heart began to beat with quick, uneven thuds.

'But — I'm feeling fine,' she said in a jerky voice and with heightened colour. 'Please, Robert, won't you let me try to forget my — health? If I felt ill, or unable to do things, I would tell you, really I would. I — '

'I'm sorry, Ray,' he interrupted, 'but I have my duty to do. I don't want to actually forbid you, so I ask you to be reasonable. Now, are you going to be a

162

sensible girl?' Rose thought quickly. She must play for time. Swiftly her eyes darted to his face, and — her heart seemed to stand still. For once more she had glimpsed that cold, implacable purpose behind his almost colourless eyes before the lids were lowered. 'Purpose, what purpose?' Rose thought, and it was as if an icy hand were squeezing her heart. She did not know; and was afraid to pursue her thoughts any further.

'Very well, Robert,' she heard herself saying quietly. 'Perhaps you are right.' He smiled at her almost paternally.

'That's better,' he said. 'Do you mind if we have our meal a little early? I have a particularly heavy session this evening. I'm sorry to have to leave you, Ray, but on the other hand, an early night will do you good after your full day. You're looking quite pale and tired.' Rose sipped her sherry. Plans were maturing in her mind.

'Yes,' she agreed placidly. 'I shall probably turn in after dinner; it's been

163

quite a day, after all. I'll just go and telephone Laurie that he must make it another evening.' Stanton looked at her, then nodded.

Rose put down her glass and went to the telephone at the rear of the big square hall; she had no intention of telephoning Laurie. Instead, she waited for a moment or two, then slipped quietly up to her room to bath and change. Her heart was still beating quickly and uneasily. It was no use pretending any longer that she was not afraid of Robert Stanton. His eyes struck terror into her heart. Unreasoning terror? Perhaps. Without knowing any of the circumstances, Rose's instinct, sharpened by the life of hazard she had led, told her that this man intended — somehow — to get Ray's money. Somehow? And now Rose faced the question squarely. What did she mean by 'somehow'? Yes, if not by marrying her, and so gaining control of it, then how? By some other means. And that could only mean — ? But still she flinched from the monstrous conclusion.

Rose never quite knew how she got through dinner that night with Robert Stanton. They were alone, as Alison had gone to a small friend's birthday party. But Rose's though past life now stood her in good stead. She had faced tricky situations before without turning a hair, and somehow she managed to do it now, and the dinner came to an end at last. As soon as Stanton had gone, bidding Rose a pleasant good night, she went to the lounge, and waited to hear the car leave. Alison came in almost at the same moment, but soon went up to bed. Now was Rose's chance to slip out of the house, and without wasting a minute she shrugged herself into her coat, picked up her handbag, and slipped out at the side door. She was afraid she would be very late, but a comforting warmth spread through her at the thought that, whatever the time, Laurie would be there waiting. And as Rose reached the entrance to the 'Miromar' she saw him standing inside.

'Ray,' he said, coming forward

eagerly to meet her, and taking both her hands in his, 'I'm so glad you are late, too; I've only just arrived, and I was worried at the thought of you waiting here alone.' Rose felt a glad lightening of the heart as she met the glance of his eyes. She smiled, and resolved to put all her nagging worries behind her for this evening at least.

'What makes you think I would have waited?' she asked teasingly. Laurie gave her an answering smile.

'Wouldn't you, Ray?' he murmured as he slipped his hand through her arm and led her forward. Rose could feel herself blushing just like an ordinary well-brought-up young woman, instead of the child of fortune that she was — or had been. She nodded her head and Laurie looked down into her face and pressed her arm.

'Come along, let's eat,' he said. 'We haven't much time, unfortunately. It was good of you to come at such short notice, Ray.'

The two walked side by side into the

brightly-lighted dining-room. Laurie looked closely into Ray's face, opened his lips as if to say something, then appeared to change his mind. As Rose took her place at the table she suddenly laughed and looked across at him.

'Do you mind if I don't have dinner?' she asked. 'You see — ' And then told him that Stanton had forbidden her to go out. Laurie looked concerned for a moment, then smiled uncertainly.

'Well — I don't know — ' he said, then grinned. 'He is certainly taking his position as guardian seriously. But, really, Ray, an evening like this can't possibly do any harm. Does he make many restrictions?' Rose nodded. 'Well, why don't you have a — talk with him? He surely can see that a young girl like you cannot be expected to — to, well, not make friends of her own age and — get about a bit.'

Rose nodded again without looking at him. If only it was as simple as that, she thought, and turned the talk into other channels.

'Well, look, have some soup and the sweet,' Laurie suggested with a smile. Rose agreed and started to tell him about the afternoon's car trip.

'So he doesn't mind you going out with him,' Laurie remarked thoughtfully, and Rose was glad that at that moment the waiter arrived with the first course. After that it seemed that in no time at all Laurie was looking at his watch and saying regretfully:

'Well, much as I hate to say it, Ray, I shall have to be going. I'll see you home first, then — '

'No,' Rose interrupted, and Laurie looked surprised. 'No, don't, it's not far, and I shall enjoy the short walk back, really.' He looked at her uncertainly, then stretched out a hand and laid it over hers on the table.

'Ray dear,' he asked, 'is something the matter? Apart from Stanton's annoying restrictions, I mean?'

She looked at his anxious face, and felt the comforting pressure of his hand over hers, and in that moment Rose would have given anything in the world to have been able to tell him the whole sad, shameful story. Not only the deception, but her present nameless fears and suspicions of Robert Stanton. But she knew that she could not bring herself to do it. To watch the dawning horror and contempt in his eyes as he realised the kind of girl she really was — no, it would be more than Rose could bear. Would he really believe in her suspicions of Stanton? Did she really believe it herself? Away from the fearful terror of her own thoughts; sitting here close to Laurie and feeling the simple directness and honesty of his whole personality reaching out to her, Rose found it almost easy to banish her fears. It's all too fantastic, she thought, and smiled brightly into Laurie's watchful face.

'Nothing's the matter,' she said. 'Well, apart from that annoying old fuss-pot. That's the reason really why I'd rather go home alone — just in case he's snooping around.' Laurie still looked doubtful.

'But, Ray, in that case — ' he began, but she cut in on him impatiently.

'No, no, no, Laurie. Let me — '

'All right, all right,' he interrupted, laughing, and rising to his feet. Then, as he helped her on with her coat, he added softly, 'When am I going to see you again?'

Rose's heart leapt at his words, then sank into sudden hopelessness as she remembered her resolve to go away. She knew that she could not go on like this much longer. Apart from her shadowy fears of Stanton, there was her newly-awakened conscience which now gave her no peace. Come what may, Rose knew that she had to clear herself of this load of guilt.

'I'll say good night here, Laurie,' Rose said, stopping at a quiet, dim corner at the end of the road. 'But I'll ring you soon — very soon.'

'You will, honest?' and suddenly she was in his arms. Oh, the joy of feeling his eager lips on hers; and the comfort of his strongly-clasping arms round her waist. 'Good night, my dear,' he whispered. 'Let it be — very soon.'

Rose slept little that night. She had slipped noiselessly in by the back door, and streaked swiftly up to her room. Robert would think she was in bed anyway, but she was taking no chances. Just before getting into bed, she stared for a moment at the door. Should she lock it? No, that would be the first concession to panic. Rose shrugged her shoulders, got into bed and snapped off the light.

She stared wide-eyed into the darkness. 'The sooner I decide just what to do, the better,' she thought bleakly. 'Oh, what a fool, and a rotten fool, I have been. If only I could put the clock back — just for a few months, but I can't, I'm trapped. I *must* get away from here — but where to go, and — what about Laurie?' Rose clenched her hands impotently as she thought of him and his good-night kiss. 'I love him,' her unhappy thoughts ran. 'The first man I have ever really and truly loved, and I don't know *why* I feel like this. He's ordinary; at least, most women would think so. There's nothing the least bit outstanding about him — and yet, why *do* people love the ones they do? Even they cannot say why. We certainly don't love others for what they look like, or what they do or say, or even for what we think they are. No, we just love them, and that's how it is with me — and Laurie, for I know that he does love me. Is *his* love like that, I wonder?'

Could she tell him the whole dreadful, sordid story, right from the beginning? Even if it killed his love, he might help her to find a way out of the tangle she had made of her life. Could she bring herself to do it? She need say nothing of her suspicions of Stanton, which might be just fantasies, after all. Could she confess to Laurie and ask his help and advice? Rose thought for a moment, then gave a sudden shiver and shook her head from side to side. No, she could not do it. Why should she shift her guilty burden on to his shoulders? Hers was the guilt and the shame, and somehow *she* must solve the problem. Rose's distracted thoughts now came full circle. 'I must leave here; there is no other way out. Laurie will forget me, and I shall forget him.' It was like death to think like that, but it was the only logical conclusion, and Rose knew it. 'I'll go to London,' she thought feverishly. 'I'll get a job and send a written confession to the lawyers. Will it mean prison?' she wondered, and shivered uncontrollably. 'But perhaps if I return the money already spent, and it's not very much, and I still have some of my own, perhaps — ' But in the middle of this last disjointed thought — Rose fell asleep.

She saw nothing of Stanton till the evening of the following day. She had deliberately kept out of his way, and had taken lunch in town where she had telephoned Alison to say that she would not be back till afternoon. The child met Rose on her return with evidence of joy and relief. She rushed to her and put both arms round her waist.

'Oh, Ray,' she said, and gave her a quick squeeze. 'I — I thought you weren't coming back. I'm glad you did. Can we go for a little walk?'

'Why, yes, of course,' Rose said, laughing a little, but quite touched at the child's evident affection for her. She suddenly realised that she herself was quite fond of Alison. The two had their walk, and then went upstairs to make ready for the evening meal.

Robert Stanton was already in the dining-room when Rose entered. She was feeling calm, almost numb now, for she had reached her decision. Rose had decided that she would leave for London the following day. She would tell Mrs Branksome after Robert had left the house that she would not be in for lunch, and then slip out with her suitcase. In that way, Stanton would not know till the evening that his ward had gone. Alison had already told her that she was going back to school in the evening to rehearse for the Christmas play. Rose dare not allow herself to think of Laurie.

'Well, stranger,' Stanton greeted Rose. 'And where did you get to at lunch-time?' Though his tone was jocular, there was a thin, tight look about his lips that made Rose feel nervous.

'I — I went to the library,' she said, sitting down in her usual place. 'Then I got interested in the Reference Section, and — I forgot all about the time.'

'You're looking tired,' he said abruptly. 'I'd better give you some tablets to take.' He took a small phial from his waistcoat pocket and unscrewed the top. 'Take them now.' He shook two out on to the palm of his hand, and reached for Rose's glass. But before his hand touched it, they all heard the strident call of the telephone: and almost immediately came Mrs Branksome's footsteps crossing the hall. 'Take them in a little water,' Stanton continued, and reached for the jug. But Rose was before him, and as the housekeeper came into the room, she was pouring water into the glass.

'It's a call from Professor Ross for you, Mr Stanton,' Mrs Branksome said, and he immediately got to his feet.

'The call I've been waiting for,' he muttered, then dropped the small white tablets into Rose's glass and left the room.

'What are they, Ray?' Alison asked, leaning forward over the table. The next instant her own glass of water toppled from the table's edge and fell to the polished floor. 'Oh!' said the child, her face going white. She bent down and stared at the mess of glass and water.

'Never mind, darling,' Rose said, bending swiftly; then, unnoticed by the agitated child, she silently tipped over her own glass to join the wet pool on the table. 'It's only water, it will soon dry.'

Inwardly Rose was blessing this small accident. It had given her the opportunity to dispose of the water in her own glass — and those little white tablets. They may be just what they were supposed to be — sedatives, but she did not trust them — or Stanton. 'Don't touch the pieces,' she now said to Alison. 'You might cut yourself. We'll ask Mrs Branksome to clear it away when she comes in.'

'Oh, no,' the child said agitatedly. 'Please ask her before Daddy — ' But at that moment Stanton returned. He took in the scene at a glance, then he looked at Alison.

'I'm — I'm sorry, Daddy,' she muttered in a trembling voice. 'I — I couldn't help it, I — '

'Couldn't help it!' Rose looked at him quickly, and saw the cruel set to his lips. 'Surely a girl of your age — go straight up to bed for being so careless, go along, at once.' Rose stared at him indignantly, then at the child; and suddenly she was shocked and horrified at the expression of fear on Alison's face as she glanced at her father before scrambling to her feet.

'Yes, Daddy, I'm sorry.' The words were almost inaudible as she almost ran to the door. Rose's heart swelled with sympathy for the child, and indignation at the father; and she knew that what she had half-suspected for some time was true: this little girl was frightened of her father.

'Weren't you a bit hard on her?' she asked as the door closed behind the child. He made an impatient movement and sat down. 'It was an accident, after all, and — '

'Filthy mess,' he muttered, and got up again to ring the bell. Mrs Branksome came in, and after taking in what had happened sent Millie, the small kitchenmaid, in to clean up the mess on the floor and table. 'I shall have to go in a few minutes,' he said to Rose after the girl had gone again. 'Will you — '

'Certainly,' Rose said, not looking at him. 'I shall have a quiet evening reading my library book.'

As soon as she heard Stanton leave the house, Rose went in search of Alison, after first instructing Mrs

Branksome to take a tray to the child's room. She found the little girl in bed, crying miserably into her pillows.

'Hello,' Rose said, sitting down on the side of the bed. 'Cheer up, old girl. I expect your parent had had a busy morning, and was feeling tired and fed-up at having to turn out again in the evening. Look, Mrs Branksome's going to bring you something on a tray, and I'm going to sit here with you while you eat it.' She put a tentative hand on the child's shoulder. Alison turned suddenly and, with a fresh access of sobs, flung both arms round Rose's neck.

'Oh, Ray,' she sobbed, and Rose could feel the violent trembling of the small body. 'I — I didn't mean to do it; I couldn't help it. Oh, Ray, please, please, Ray, don't ever go away, don't leave me here — alone.'

Instinctively, Rose's arms tightened round the child as she tried to look into the tear-stained face. What did Alison mean? How did she know that that was what Rose was planning to do. But of course the child knew nothing; how could she? She was just upset, and tomorrow it would all be forgotten. In any case, and here Rose half-turned away from the child's pleading face, it was no concern of hers. Alison was nothing to her; she was certainly not *her* responsibility. The little girl seemed to sense what was going on in Rose's mind, for she stopped weeping and whispered:

'You're not — going away, are you, Ray?' Rose turned her eyes away and half-opened her lips to give an evasive answer, but then she hesitated. No, no, she decided, she was done with lies and deceit. From now on it was to be the truth, and so — there was a long silence between the two girls; but Alison's grip on Rose tightened and her wide eyes continued to stare imploringly into her face.

'Please, Ray,' she whispered, then added, almost inaudibly, 'I love you, Ray — ever so. Please stay here with me.' Rose had a sudden violent urge to shake herself free from the child's clinging arms. 'Oh, why the hell does this have to happen now?' she thought almost frantically. 'This kid's nothing to me; why, a few months ago I didn't even know she existed. She'll come through it; I've got no duty to her, or to anyone.'

'But is that true?' the annoyingly interfering voice inside her asked. 'Can anyone in the whole world say they have no duty to anyone else? Isn't that just the core of the Christian religion, our duty and love towards our neighbour?'

Abruptly, Rose freed herself from the child's arms and got to her feet. 'What's that to do with me?' She almost said the words aloud, and back came the answer:

'Aren't you supposed to be a Christian, or is it only a name?'

Rose made a furious little gesture of exasperation. 'I didn't choose to be anything; Christian, Baptist, Bhuddist,

Jehovah's Witness or any other of the countless sects and creeds. It's just nothing to me — this kid's nothing to me, either.' Almost against her will, Rose slowly turned and looked at the child.

'I'm sorry, Ray,' Alison said quietly, her small face queerly withdrawn and adult all at once. 'I shouldn't ask you to stay if — if you don't want to; but I *do* love you, Ray. You're so pretty — and kind.'

'Kind!' Rose thought with an unbearable twist of the heart. 'Oh, God! Kind!' Swiftly she went back to the bed and put tight comforting arms round the child.

'Don't worry any more, darling,' she whispered. 'Of course I am not going away, and — I love you, too.' There came a soft little sigh of relief from Alison, and a thought exploded in Rose's mind. 'Love one another' — so said the Christians. But — there were Christians *and* Christians, and Rose had met both kinds. Well, that's not the fault of the One who started it all. *His* teaching was quite clear. Then she grinned wryly to herself above Alison's head; I'll be climbing on to a soap-box next, Rose thought.

9

When Rose went down to breakfast the next morning she wondered if it were her imagination that Stanton gave her a quick, keen glance before turning his attention to Alison. The child seemed quite normal this morning and smiled dutifully when her father addressed her. 'I'm imagining things again,' Rose concluded impatiently. 'First the tablets, then Alison's fear of her father; I never used to be such a neurotic creature. This lazy life does not agree with me. Of course the kid was upset at being shown up like that; she's at the sensitive age.' But in spite of these eminently sensible thoughts, Rose could not shut her mind to the child's almost hysterical outburst, and the promise she herself had made. Well, what was she to do now? 'Oh, forget it,' Rose told herself silently. 'You know nothing at all about kids, you've never had anything to do with them. Why, Alison herself has probably forgotten all about it this morning.' And as if to confirm these thoughts, the child burst out laughing at some joke made by her father. Rose looked at her, but Alison's face was hidden as she bent over her bowl of cereal.

'I'll take you along to school this morning, Alison,' Stanton said. 'I'm going that way, but you must get a move on.'

'Yes, Daddy, I'm — I'm nearly finished.'

'What is your programme this morning, Ray?' Stanton's voice was casual, but as Rose looked at him she saw that he was watching her closely.

'I really haven't any plans,' she replied, in an equally casual voice. 'I guess I'll just have a lazy morning letterwriting and reading; and this afternoon Mrs Keogh has asked me to tea.' Jane Keogh was the jolly young wife of one of the housemen at the hospital.

'Good. Well, I hope you have an enjoyable time. Don't tire yourself. Ready, Alison?'

As soon as Rose was alone, her thoughts turned to Laurie. When would she see him again? Would he telephone her or should she ring him? In spite of the promise she had made the night before, Rose was feeling less desperately unhappy than she had done the previous day. In fact, she was half-inclined to scoff at herself for having a too fertile imagination. 'Such things don't happen in these days,' she told herself, but shrank from putting into words what she meant by 'such things'. Her thoughts returned to the promise she had made to Alison, and then back again to Laurie; and Rose knew that in spite of the fears and suspicions which she could not quite banish, she would have to keep her promise to the child. For to her own surprise, Rose recognised that she had a real love and concern for the little girl. Well, then, what was to be the next step? It all centred round Laurie now, and at the core of the problem there was just one tiny, irrational gleam of hope. For whatever the outcome of this big deception, which became more terrifying each day, at least she would not have to leave Farndon and never see Laurie again. Rose could not truthfully see how that helped, but — she loved him and hoped desperately that a way would present itself. In her innermost heart Rose felt that anything was better than voluntarily cutting him out of her life.

She got through her tea date with Jane Keogh, and about five minutes after she had arrived back she heard the ring of the telephone. Before anyone else could get there, Rose was at the instrument with the receiver up to her ear. Her heart thudded with mingled joy and despair as she heard his voice.

'Hello, Ray,' he said, and his voice was a caress. 'I — I hope you don't mind me ringing, but I wondered — if you have nothing better to do — well, er — ' Rose laughed softly.

'Don't be so modest,' she said. 'I can't think of anything better to do than to go out, anywhere — with you.' She knew she was being reckless, but thought: 'I might as well take what happiness I can — while I can.' 'Tonight?'

'Would you, Ray?' His voice was eager, but diffident at the same time. 'I'm afraid I have only a couple of hours free, but — I thought we might go for a drive into the country and stop for a drink at a cosy little pub I know. I'd like to ask you for dinner, but — '

'Oh, but what you suggest sounds fun,' Rose said, breaking in on him, and busily planning to herself just how she would arrange things. Yes, she decided, it would be much easier to slip out after dinner than before. She could think of an excuse for going to bed early.

'About nine, Laurie?' Rose suggested. 'That all right?'

'Couldn't be better,' he replied. 'And how are you, Ray?'

'Right on top of the world right now,' Rose said, casting all caution to the winds; then, at sound of Stanton's car coming up the drive, she added quickly, 'Must go now, Laurie. Till tonight.'

She was out and half-way up the stairs before Robert came in. 'Oh, lovely to be seeing Laurie again,' she thought. 'Only another two hours to wait.'

Dinner passed off quite pleasantly. Robert was in a genial mood, and both Rose and Alison enjoyed the meal. However, Rose knew that she must prepare the ground for her evening out. So when Alison suggested a card game of some sort Rose smiled apologetically and asked to be excused.

'I've had quite a day,' she said, looking appealingly at the little girl. 'I think I will have a quiet evening, and go to bed early. Would you mind, dear?'

'Why no, of course not, Ray. Can I get you anything before you go?' Rose shook her head, feeling suddenly guilty and mean. The sensation surprised her considerably. 'What's come over me?' she wondered. 'Six months ago I'd have thought nothing of the convenient little lie to suit myself. Gosh, if this goes on I shall be sprouting wings next!'

Quite soon after this, Alison said her good nights and went upstairs. Rose stole a glance at her wristwatch. Stanton got up and walked over to the drinks cabinet. He looked at Rose over his shoulder, and she noticed that his pale eyes were a trifle bloodshot. 'He drinks too much,' Rose suddenly thought.

'What will you have, Ray?' he asked, and lifted an eyebrow. Rose shook her head and passed a hand across her forehead.

'Robert, would you mind if I went to bed now?' she asked. 'I've got a bit of a headache.' He frowned and came across to her.

'Or is it the thought of an evening spent in my company?' he said in a nasty tone of voice. 'You need not worry; I have to go out again quite soon.' He paused, then added abruptly, 'Have you a temperature, do you think?'

'No. Oh, no.' She shook her head quickly, glad that he had not waited for a reply to his previous remark. 'It's just that — well, perhaps I overdid it today.' 'It's going to be easy,' Rose was thinking. 'I shall just wait till he goes.'

'Well, a good night's sleep should put that right.' He walked over to her side and stood looking down into her face. Rose was uneasily conscious of his nearness, and suddenly he laughed softly and put his hand round her shoulder. 'Good night, my dear,' he murmured. 'Sweet dreams.'

Rose waited breathlessly in her own room till she heard the car drive away. Then, silently and swiftly, and forgetting even to put on a wrap, she was down the stairs and out of the house at the side door. She did not want the housekeeper or the little maid to hear her departure in case they mentioned it to Stanton on his return. The doors were never locked till midnight, but she was taking no chances.

Rose found Laurie waiting for her at the arranged meeting place. He greeted her with a boyish beaming smile. 'Let me look at you before we start,' he said, then made a sudden swipe above Rose's shoulder. 'Yes, you look more beautiful every time I see you. Damn, the mosquitoes are out in force tonight. Did you have a nip?' as her hand clapped sharply down on to her bare arm. 'Come along, it's wise to get moving.' He tucked a hand through her arm and led her to the waiting car.

Rose's face was still blushing from Laurie's first remark and again she had the desire to laugh at the thought that she, tough and worldly-wise as she was, should be blushing like a schoolgirl at the ordinary common-place remark of this very ordinary young man. She gave the bite on her arm another rub.

'I didn't know you had mosquitoes

in England,' Rose said, and Laurie laughed.

'Well, it's a sign of good weather over here,' he said. 'But don't rub it, Ray.'

Laurie drove for a time through the quiet country roads, and then drew up outside a small pub. There was a wooden trestle table and a couple of benches outside. Inside was a small curved bar, a padded bench running round the walls, and a few tables and chairs set out at intervals. Rose sat down at one of the tables while Laurie went to the bar to collect their drinks. He returned with two tankards of ale and sat down opposite Rose.

'Cigarette?' he asked, holding out his case. Rose took one and Laurie produced his lighter. He leaned back and sighed with satisfaction. 'I've had a busy day,' he remarked. 'You don't mind — this, Ray? and he gave a comprehensive glance at his surroundings.

'I think it's fun,' Rose said, smiling at him across the table. She looked about her with lively interest; it was something quite new to her. There was nothing quite like this in India. Rose looked towards the bar, where mine host was cosily discussing the latest cricket scores with a couple of farmery-looking men in tweed jackets and leather gaiters. At the next table to theirs sat a man and a woman with mugs of beer in front of them and not a word being exchanged. Married couple, Rose thought with unconscious cynicism. Her glance passed on to where two or three long-haired youths were engaged in a rather noisy game of darts. All so ordinary and every-day; yet a wave of sheer happiness engulfed Rose as she brought her gaze back to Laurie's face. Then a thought struck her. *This* was not what she had imagined as the happiness that could be hers when she had recklessly taken on another girl's identity. Wonderful clothes, furs, jewels, an exciting and sophisticated social life, and eventually a satisfactory marriage with a handsome, distinguished man.

Yes, that was the future Rose had imagined for herself. But this — this was just the ordinary life of the ordinary hard-working citizen. And this, Rose realised at long last, was the life she wanted. But what had brought about this bewildering change? Rose looked straight into Laurie's blue eyes with their expression of directness and simplicity; and again the memory of the quiet lake in the hills of Southern India came to her; and she knew, with mingled feelings of rapture and despair, that at last she had found the thing for which she had been looking then — and for ever since. The meaning of life. Love, true love between a man and a woman and the perfect harmony which follows. That was what Rose had longed for, without knowing it. Pain stabbed at her heart; pain so sharp and desperate that she almost cried out, for she knew that she could never tell Laurie the truth about herself. Her very love for him turned her into a coward. And yet, tell him she must, now that she had made up her mind not to leave Farndon — and Alison.

'You're looking very thoughtful, darling,' Laurié said, then looked bashful as his eyes met hers. There was a silence between them, then Rose said softly:

'It's the first time you ever called me that.'

'I know. Do you mind?'

'No — ' Her voice ended on a rising note, and Laurie looked at her questioningly.

'Shall we go, Ray?' he asked. 'Or would you care for another drink?' Rose shook her head.

'No,' she said, 'I'm quite ready.' Laurie led the way out, and they walked towards the car. In silence Laurie started off, but they had not gone far before he turned into a quiet side road and presently drew up on to a grass verge. Rose's heartbeats quickened with mingled emotions as Laurie turned to her and looked into her shadowy face.

'Darling,' he said, then gave a little laugh. 'And that's the second time.' He felt for her hand. 'Ray, I — I wonder if you know just how I feel about you. Right from the time that I first saw you, on the ship — I knew that — Oh, Ray, I — I love you, and want you to marry me. I know it's awful presumption on my part, but — '

'Please, please, Laurie,' Rose interrupted in an agitated voice. 'Of course it is not presumption. I — ' Then she stopped. She was exalted yet miserable at the same time. She knew that she should have stopped Laurie saying it — but it was so sweet to hear those words from the man that she loved with all her heart. And now, what was she to say to him? Rose longed to say that she loved him, and wanted nothing more in the world than to be his wife, but — she could not; not without first telling him the whole sordid truth about herself. Rose's heart was full to bursting as the silence lengthened between them.

'Ray,' Laurie murmured at last, and turned her face gently up to his. There was a pause, and then Rose felt his lips on hers, and dazedly gave herself up to the delight of this, his first real kiss of love. 'Darling — ' he said softly after a minute or two. 'Say that you, too — ' But panic was now possessing Rose. She felt like a trapped animal with the Elysian fields stretching before her, but unable to free herself and enter them.

'I — I don't know,' she almost gasped, then drew abruptly away from him. 'I — I must think. I — I, you see, it's a big step to take, and, and — ' She stopped and Laurie cut in quietly.

'Why, of course, Ray,' he said. 'I know that I'm not much of a catch in the marriage market — ' He gave a little laugh. 'For someone as lovely as you, I mean. Perhaps I shouldn't have spoken at all, but I — '

'Oh, please, please, Laurie,' Rose said, twisting her hands together in an agony of remorse and indecision. 'Don't misunderstand me. Please don't think that I — that I — ' Laurie looked into her agitated face and pressed the hand nearest to him.

'Now don't upset yourself, Ray,' he said quietly. 'I — don't quite understand, but, well — I suppose I made a mistake. I somehow thought that you, too — '

'Oh, I do, I do,' Rose almost wailed. 'But — well, it's all so difficult. I — I shall have to think things out, and — ' Her voice trailed away as Laurie turned and switched on the engine.

'Let's drop the subject, shall we?' he suggested almost casually as he started up the engine. 'Anyway, how could I expect a girl like you, with just everything, to look at an ordinary chap like me?' He smiled sideways at her, but Rose knew that he was deeply hurt.

'But — ' she began, then stopped. What was there to say? What could she say to him? A heavy silence hung between them as the car gained speed. Rose was so sunk in misery that she found it impossible to say a word. Laurie started to make a little light conversation but it soon petered out and they were both thankful when the journey was over. At Rose's request, Laurie had stopped the car at the entrance to the drive as she did not want to risk anyone hearing her return. Quietly, Laurie got out and went round to the other side. He opened the door and waited for Rose to climb out.

'Ray, dear,' he said, and placed both hands on her shoulders. 'Somehow, I don't think you are very happy. I just want to say that if there's anything I can do, just tell me, won't you?' Rose's bursting heart seemed to rise to her throat and almost choke her.

'Thank you,' she gulped in muffled tones; hesitated for a moment, then turned and almost ran up the drive. As she approached the side door Rose slowed down and tiptoed soundlessly forward. She had seen that there was a light still on in Stanton's study and now, with infinite care, she softly turned the handle and crept forward. The study was at the other side of the wide hall, and from the side door a narrow staircase led direct to the upstairs rooms. Rose felt fairly confident that even if Robert happened to come out of his study he would not be able to see her noiselessly ascending the back staircase. However, as Rose started up she stumbled on the first step and at the slight sound she made, the study door was immediately thrown open, and Stanton came swiftly round the foot of the main staircase, switching on the light as he did so. Rose stood motionless, clutching the stair rail, and staring at Robert Stanton. His face looked flushed and puffy, and she saw that he had been drinking.

'Where have you been?' he asked in a thick, level voice which struck a chill to Rose's heart. With an effort she dragged her eyes from his almost expressionless face and looked down at her feet. It was then that she saw the tennis racquet half on and half off the first step of the stairs. Left there carelessly by Alison? Perhaps; perhaps not. Rose felt her heartbeats beginning to quicken, and she made a desperate effort to calm herself. 'Don't be a cowardly fool,' she whispered to herself soundlessly. 'You are an adult, you must stand up to this man.' But she felt again like a trapped animal; but this time it was infinitely more terrifying because she did not know if it was in her imagination or not.

'Well?' Stanton said again. Rose forced herself to look at him, into the flushed face, and into the cold, colourless eyes — and shrank back.

'I've — been out,' she said, trying to make her voice sound normal. Stanton came a step nearer.

'I know that,' he said roughly. A wave of almost hysterical anger shook Rose suddenly. What right had Robert Stanton to speak to her like this? True, he was her guardian, or so he thought, but that did not make her his slave. 'I ask you again, Ray. Where have you been — and with whom?'

'Oh, very well,' Rose said, with the courage of desperation. 'I have been out for a drive — with Laurie Drake.' She stared straight at him as she spoke, but if she had hoped for a flicker of expression from that cold, enigmatic face she was disappointed. 'There is nothing strenuous in that, is there, so — ' Stanton walked slowly and deliberately towards her, and Rose felt her spurious courage beginning to ebb. She saw again that he was very drunk.

'My dear Ray,' he said in a soft but blurred sort of voice, and stopping just in front of her. 'Your tiredness disappeared very quickly. I confess I was surprised to say the least when I went to your room at about nine-thirty to see if you wanted anything — a hot drink, I thought — to find that the bird had flown. Why did you not tell me that you were planning to go out?'

'Because you'd have tried to stop me,' Rose blurted, beginning to feel at a terrible disadvantage. 'You — you always do.' Stanton stared down into her strained white face, then laughed.

'Come and have a drink,' he suggested suddenly and surprisingly. He slipped a hand through Rose's arm, and drew her unwillingly forward. 'We don't want Mrs B. to hear this conversation, do we? Now — ' He pushed her suddenly into an armchair. 'What will you have?'

'Thanks, but — I don't want anything,' Rose muttered, fidgeting uneasily in the chair. She rubbed again at the itching mosquito bite on her upper arm, then struggled to her feet. 'Please, Robert, I'd rather go to bed now.'

'Oh, but it's quite early still,' he said in a pleasantly conversational sort of way, even though the words were still slightly slurred. He laughed softly, and added, 'Come and watch an experiment I'm working on — in the laboratory.' He suddenly took Rose's arm in a firm grip, and her heart began to beat madly as she met the glance of those pale, implacable eyes. Oh, what was he going to do — or was it just her imagination again? Rose could not be sure, and she was afraid to cross him.

'I — I think I'm rather tired,' she muttered faintly, and trying to withstand the steady pressure of his hand as he propelled her towards that sinister little room behind the stairs. Her breath came jerkily, and it was as if an icy hand was clutching at her heart. 'Please, Robert, I — '

'Here we are,' he cut in, still retaining his grip on Rose's arm. 'Now, over here.' He drew her forward. 'I'll try to explain in very simple terms. You see this little syringe — ' Rose shrank from it in vague terror. 'Well, over there you can see — ' He pointed to her left, and slightly loosened his hold on her arm. Rose looked quickly in the direction to which he nodded, and suddenly he gave an exclamation of annoyance and bent forward. Rose glanced back, wondering what had happened to annoy him, and at the same time felt a slight pricking irritation on her upper arm. Sharply she drew away from contact with Stanton and rubbed again at the mosquito bite on her arm.

'What is the matter?' he asked, looking closely into her face. 'What's wrong with your arm?'

'No, it's just a mosquito bite,' Rose said, some of her confidence returning as Stanton made no move to come nearer to her again. 'I'm — rather allergic to them.' She rubbed at the small swelling again. He stared at her, and a curious little smile began to play around his lips.

'Better let me see it,' he suggested. 'There's sure to be something here — that we could apply.' Rose's vague but still terrifying fears began to return.

'No,' she said sharply and backing away from him towards the door. 'It's nothing really; just a bit irritating.'

'Come along now, Ray,' he said soothingly. 'Let me have a look at it; won't take a minute,' and he suddenly grasped her arm and pushed the light sleeve up. 'Now, where is it? Ah, yes, I see. I think just a little dab of — ' But Rose pulled her arm sharply away from him and reached the door.

'No,' she almost snapped at him. 'It — it'll be all right in the morning, Robert. No, I don't want anything put on it.' Why did she have this feeling of dread, Rose wondered. She looked at Stanton over her shoulder, halfexpecting, and dreading, that he would follow her, but he did not. Instead he just smiled at her; a curious smile, Rose thought, almost triumphant. But why should Robert Stanton be feeling triumphant? He was making no more effort to keep her, had apparently forgotten about the experiment he was going to show her, and had asked no more questions about her evening out with Laurie. So why did she have this heavy feeling of dread? Rose reached the door, then took another glance back at Stanton and saw that he was still smiling.

'Very well, my dear,' he said quite pleasantly. 'You seem to be allergic to remedies, also; but if that is how you feel — ' He shrugged. 'Perhaps bed is the best place for you, after all. Good night, my dear. Sleep well.'

Rose stared at him from the door. What an extraordinary man, she was thinking, but — mentally she shook her head in bewilderment and began to wonder if there was something wrong with her own mind. 'God! I shall have to do something soon,' she thought, 'before I go completely nuts.'

'Good night, Robert,' Rose muttered, and as she hurried from the room she heard his soft little laugh following her. That night Rose locked her bedroom door.

10

Once inside her own room and with the door locked, Rose sank limply on to the side of her bed. Her head ached and she clasped it with hot hands. What was she afraid of? 'Come on, out with it,' the voice inside her suddenly said. 'Whatever it is, bring it out into the open.' Rose stared dumbly in front of her and waited for the answer. 'Isn't it this?' the quiet voice continued. 'You are wondering *why* Robert Stanton asked you to marry him; because he has fallen in love with you?' Almost without knowing it, Rose shook her head. 'No,' she replied soundlessly, 'he just wants my money.' 'Yours?' came the voice again, and she cringed almost as if she had been struck. 'It is Robert Stanton's money — and what are you going to do about that?' The voice gave her no peace. 'Oh, God!' Rose thought wildly.

'If only I could hand it over to him, the lot, now. But how can I — without telling the whole sordid story? What can I do? What can I do?'

Rose's distracted thoughts began all over again. 'Robert Stanton wants this money, and he is determined to get it — somehow. *I* want to get rid of it, and as soon as possible. But why does he want this money so badly? He is well-off, or so Ray had said.' But Rose had an idea that she'd been wrong as she thought of the many signs of neglect in the house. 'Is it something to do with his experiments,' she wondered, 'and does he need a great deal of money in order to continue with them? They are his big interest, I know that.' Rose licked her dry lips. Surely there was something she could do. Couldn't she offer to give or to lend him the money? She'd gladly give it all, and so escape from this nightmare of guilt and dread. But what of Stanton? Wouldn't he wonder why, and ask questions? He was no fool. A revulsion of feeling shook Rose. No, no, no. She beat her hands violently on her knees. Even if it were possible, she could not do it. She'd got to get clear of all this deception, even though it meant an open scandal and perhaps prison. She must free herself of all the lies and sham, and become a *real* person again. Even though it meant losing Laurie and being cast out homeless and penniless? Well, she'd been homeless and penniless before, Rose thought bleakly. Yes, she could cope with that, but — to lose Laurie! Could she bear it, now that she knew that he loved her and wanted her for his wife? A heavy silence descended upon her, then slowly she nodded her head. Yes, she could even do that, she would have to, wouldn't she? Perhaps in time — well, time was supposed to heal all wounds —

Quite suddenly Rose broke out into a cold sweat as a wave of nausea struck her. What was the matter now? Was the strain and stress beginning to get her down? Then into her shrinking mind, like the slide of a venomous snake, came a thought, a recollection of Stanton standing close beside her in the laboratory — and the faint prick on the soft flesh of her upper arm. 'Oh, God!' Rose thought in a new panic. 'Why do I have these awful thoughts?' But with cold, clumsy fingers she pushed the light sleeve aside and looked at her arm. Yes, that was the spot where she had felt, or thought she felt, the tiny prick, but — it was also the place where she had rubbed at the mosquito bite. With dry lips she stared down at her arm. There was a redness and a slight swelling. Of course it is the mosquito bite, Rose thought but — why then was she feeling so sick and faint? Instinct drove Rose to her feet and she started walking about the room. Wasn't that what people did when they thought they might have been — Rose's thoughts stopped dead as one clenched hand came up against her mouth. 'Stop it, stop it,' she told herself, but continued to walk waveringly about the room. She began to lose count of time, but the sickness and faintness gradually became too much for her and at last she sank, only half-conscious, on to her bed.

It was broad daylight when Rose awoke. She felt limp and exhausted, but the sickness and faintness had mercifully gone. Recollection rushed over her, and she sat up and stared down at her arm. The swelling and redness had almost disappeared, and again Rose thought, 'What a neurotic fool I am! I'll have to pull myself together. This can't go on much longer.'

At breakfast Robert gave her a pleasant good morning. His face showed no signs of a hangover, and the events of the previous night appeared to be forgotten. Alison smiled brightly at Rose and asked if she were going shopping that morning. Everything seemed so normal and ordinary that Rose thought again, 'What an imaginative idiot I am. It's a guilty conscience, of course, and the sooner I decide what exactly I am going to do, the better.'

The day passed peacefully in the usual pleasant if rather dull routine till the evening, and then — something happened that brought back all Rose's vague fears and misgivings in full flood. They had all three watched television — Alison being allowed an extra half-hour to watch a special programme — and then, at about ten-thirty, Rose and Robert had exchanged good nights and gone to their respective rooms.

Rose started to undress, then noticed that the curtains at the window were billowing inwards. Millie's forgotten again, Rose thought as she went to close them. The windows were diamond paned and opened outwards. She stepped on to the smooth oriental rug which was always placed just under the window, braced her thighs against the rather low sill and leaned outward. Then — in one terrifying second her feet shot back and up into the air. With a gasp, Rose clutched at the outside of the sill, and felt the weight of her body sag forward. Gasping with terror, she doubled herself up like a jack-knife, and only just in time. Her knees hooked themselves on to the inside of the window sill, and then slowly and laboriously she inched herself back over the sill and into the room. Weak with shock, she sank down on to the rug, and felt it move again beneath her. After a moment or two Rose got to her feet and stared down at the rug. Then, stepping carefully, she bent and twitched it to one side. Rose stared at the floor beneath and her heart seemed to slowly freeze. Was the floor just under the window always polished to such a pitch of perfection? Well, she'd never noticed it before. Her eyes travelled on to the rest of the floor, but it was covered almost completely by carpet except for a narrow border running all round the room. Rose walked round, studying the border, then compared it with the square of parquet flooring under the rug. She could come to no conclusion, but it did nothing to relieve her heavy feeling of dread. After a long time she completed her undressing and got into bed. But not to sleep. Her thoughts jostled one against the other. Was this another trick of her sick imagination, or was it — ? She shook her head wearily from side to side. She just did not know, but she was rapidly approaching a point where she knew that she could not bear it alone much longer. She lay there wide-eyed hour after hour, and in the early morning Rose came to her fateful decision. Come what may, she would confess all to Laurie, the whole sordid story — and she would ask his help. There was no one else to whom she could turn. Rose knew that she risked losing his love, but it was a risk that had to be taken. She had toyed first with the idea of confessing all to the lawyers; but the mere prospect made her shudder. Rose thought that by telling the whole story to Laurie there was just the faint hope that, in spite of the shock and horror he would no doubt feel, he might think of a way of avoiding legal action. 'Perhaps,' she thought desperately, 'if I pay back every penny, and I *could* do that as I still have some of my own and I spent very little of the other, it would all be settled quietly.' It was a forlorn hope, Rose knew, but she could think of no other.

When Rose came down to breakfast feeling more dead than alive, Robert Stanton had already left and Alison was just finishing. She seemed to be excited about something.

'Got something to tell you, Ray,' she said. 'Guess what.'

'I'm not at my brightest this morning,' Rose said, pouring herself a cup of coffee. 'You tell me.' She tried to infuse some interest into her voice as she smiled across the table at the child.

'I'm going to boarding school next term. I'm thrilled, Ray. Of course I shall miss you, but there'll be the holidays, won't there?'

'Of course. I think it's a fine idea, and you'll have the company of other girls.' Rose was really glad to hear this news. Her promise to Alison had weighed heavily upon her, but now — it would not matter much longer. But why was Robert Stanton doing this? A cold finger pressed for a moment on her heart. Months alone in the house with him — or so he thought. Never. Rose shook her head silently, and decided that as soon as Alison was out of the way she would telephone Laurie, and then — For a moment her heart failed her, but only for a moment. For Rose knew that she had come to the end of her endurance.

Ten minutes later she had the telephone receiver in her hand and was dialling his number. Rose's heart was beating in her throat and almost choking her; and then a cool, impersonal voice informed her that Doctor Drake was out on a case and it was not known when he would be back. Feeling quite weak with disappointment, Rose wandered back into the hall and almost ran into Stanton. He looked at her silently, then said in a coldly impersonal voice:

'I'd like a word with you, Ray. D'you mind coming into the study for a moment?' Her heart gave an uneasy jerk. Everything about him these days made Rose feel vaguely terrified and uneasy. But she followed him in, and tried to appear calm and collected.

'I have been examining your medical documents,' he went on, waving her to a chair and then seating himself behind his desk, 'and I think perhaps a certain treatment might be beneficial. But before that some tests would have to be made. When could you go up to the hospital? This morning? I think I could arrange it with Dr Lowther.' He looked her over consideringly and Rose felt her face going stiff. But of course it was probably true — of the real Ray. Perhaps Stanton was surprised at her seeming, and continued, good health, but she knew with growing panic that she could not risk any medical examination now — not yet, Rose thought, not till she had seen Laurie.

'Oh, not today, Robert,' Rose said, managing to summon up a smile. 'I was just going out to have coffee with Jane. Couldn't you make it some other time? Perhaps — '

'Oh, very well,' he interrupted in a resigned sort of voice. 'I'll try to fix it for tomorrow, or the day after. How are you feeling in yourself?'

'Oh, not so bad,' Rose interrupted in her turn. 'I think this climate suits me better than India.'

'You certainly look well,' he remarked, reluctantly Rose thought. 'But — there must be no more late nights, Ray. Understand?'

'Late nights!' Rose laughed. 'Ten o'clock — ye gods! — late? D'you mind if I go now? I don't want to keep Jane waiting.' He nodded.

As soon as she was out of the room Rose waited till she heard Stanton go to his laboratory and close the door, and then she hurried noiselessly back to the telephone. 'Oh, let Laurie be there,' she thought desperately as she picked up the receiver once more. And this time she was not disappointed.

'Hello,' came his pleasant and well-loved voice. 'Who is — Oh, Ray, how nice to hear you, though you sound as if you have been running.' There was a worried note in his voice, and even in the midst of her agitation Rose had to fight down her feeling of exasperation. 'Thank God,' she thought, 'that come what may, I shall soon be clear of all the lies and deceit.'

'No, Laurie,' she said rapidly, 'I'm quite all right, but — I — I wondered if I could see you this evening — any time, just half an hour would do. Can you — ' There was a small pause, then:

'Why, yes — ' His voice came on a slightly surprised note. 'Yes, of course, about five? Would that suit you?' 'He sounds very formal,' Rose thought unhappily. 'Well, he will soon understand why I could not answer him last night.' She managed to reply to Laurie, and as she left the telephone Rose knew that she would again be risking Stanton's anger if he found out that she was meeting Laurie again; but it was a risk she had to take.

Rose laid her plans carefully. At lunch-time, which Alison took at school now that holidays were over, Stanton enquired casually as to what Rose was doing that afternoon.

'Oh, it's such a lovely day,' she replied, 'that I think I'll take just a short walk and have tea out.'

'A good idea,' he said. 'As long as you don't walk too far.' Rose gritted her teeth. 'I wish I could join you, but — ' He shrugged. 'It's work for me, I'm afraid.' Rose said nothing to this, and very soon he excused himself and went.

Rose waited a little longer; then quickly and quietly she went up to her room. Her heart was beating in choking thuds. In a short time now she would be meeting Laurie and would have come to the end of the road — the road of lies and deceit. Yes, come what may, she would have shed the worst of the burden — this load of secrecy.

The afternoon seemed to crawl by; but at last it was time to go, and as Rose hurried to the rendezvous she had a sudden and inexplicable lightening of the spirit. It bewildered her, for wasn't she about to confess to something that might put her in the power of the law? She was also risking the loss of Laurie's love and instead gaining his contempt and indeed horror at discovering what kind of girl she really was. And yet, she had this bewildering sense of release; a feeling almost of redemption.

Rose had one moment of panic, and wanted to turn and run when she saw that Laurie was waiting for her in his car. Her knees and hands began to tremble, and there was a sudden mist before her eyes. Laurie got out of the car and came to meet her.

'Hello, Ray,' he said quietly, then added in a voice of concern, 'Are you feeling all right?'

Rose nodded, but could find nothing to say as she climbed clumsily into the car. Laurie hesitated, then asked:

'Did you want to go anywhere in particular?'

'No.' Her voice was strained and difficult. 'Now is the moment,' she was thinking as she tried to still the violent beating of her heart. 'This is where I take the plunge. Am I being selfish in telling Laurie? But I don't know what to do; I need help and advice, and there's no one else.' 'No,' Rose said again. 'I — I don't want to go anywhere. I just want to talk to you.' Laurie smiled at her and patted her hand.

'Have you been thinking of what I said? Ray, dear, please don't let it upset you. I realise that I'm not much of a match for you. I'm not half good enough for such a lovely — '

'Stop, stop,' Rose broke in almost hysterically. 'Not good enough! Oh, Laurie, when I tell you all about myself, you'll — well — ' she shook her head despairingly, 'you won't ask me that question again; I mean, the question you asked me — last night.' Laurie stared at her in bewildered silence, then very quietly he said:

'Well, Ray, I can't imagine that happening, but — tell me what is worrying you.' He hesitated for a moment, then continued. 'I know you don't like being reminded about your heart condition, and if it is anything to do with that, Ray, then — '

'There's nothing wrong with my heart,' Rose burst out, and suddenly she had to stop herself from bursting into hysterical laughter. 'In fact, I'm as strong as a horse, and I've never had an illness in my life; and — and my name is not Ray Desmond.' Her voice was beginning to rise again, but as she forced herself to look at Laurie she saw a watchful look come into his eyes. 'Oh, heavens!' Rose thought. 'He thinks I'm crackers,' and made a supreme effort to compose herself. 'Laurie,' she said more quietly, 'Laurie — this is the truth, and I — want to tell you the whole story. It's a story of lies, and deceit, and — '

'All right, take your time.' His voice was quiet and kind, and Rose knew it was the medical man who was speaking.

'Because — ' she said, and waited to get her breath, 'I can't go on any longer; I can't live with it — for the rest of my life, and — and there was no one else I could tell it to. I — I know you'll hate me when you know what kind of person I am, and — ' She stopped and covered her face for a moment. 'Oh, Laurie, I can't bear to think of you hating me, but — ' Rose shook her head despairingly, then felt a gentle arm sliding round her shoulders.

'Ray — ' His voice was quiet and calm, almost casual. 'I could never do that. As I told you yesterday, I love you.' There was silence for a moment, then Laurie continued, 'Tell me what is the trouble — and why do you say your name is not Ray Desmond?' Rose raised her head, but could not look at him.

'It all started on the boat coming

home from India,' she said at last, almost in a whisper. 'We were — in the same cabin, and — ' And so, haltingly at first, but pouring out recklessly as she went on, the whole sordid tale was brought out and offered to Laurie's appalled ears. He had stared at Rose's half-averted face with gathering horror in his eyes, and when at last she finished he said nothing for a long moment. Rose herself could not bear to look at him; to see the disgust and aversion on his face. She had said nothing yet of her thoughts and half-suspicions of Stanton, and now wondered if it would be better not to mention these. Laurie might think her mind was deranged, and indeed Rose herself sometimes wondered if all these vague suspicions existed only in an inflamed imagination.

'Good God!' she heard Laurie whisper at last. The arm round Rose's shoulders had been quietly withdrawn, and he sat staring in front of him. Rose was also silent, weak and exhausted after her long confession. Her breath came in short, shuddering sighs. 'Good God!' Laurie said again. 'Ray — I mean — ' He looked at her briefly. 'If this is true, what are you going to do about it?'

Even in the midst of her misery Rose noticed that so far he had uttered not one single word of recrimination. But as she forced herself to look at him, she saw that his eyes were the eyes of a stranger. Though she had been prepared for this, her heart went cold and dead inside her. Yet still, beneath it all, there was the strange feeling of release, and in spite of her misery Rose knew that she had taken the first step towards redemption. But was she just being selfish, she wondered again, by burdening Laurie with this knowledge? Would he consider it his duty to —

'My God!' she heard him mutter again. 'It's — it's unbelievable. It's the sort of thing one reads in the more sensational magazines. But — why did you tell me all this, and what are you going to do?' Rose felt cold all over as she glanced for one moment at his grim face.

'I — had to tell someone,' she whispered in a voice worn husky with emotion. 'And — you seemed to be my only friend. You see, I want to finish with it all; all the lies and deceit. Oh, please believe me, Laurie, I'm not *all* bad; I just can't bear to live like this any longer. You see — ' Rose took a deep breath. 'When you told me — what you did yesterday, I — I couldn't say anything, I felt awful. But the truth is, Laurie, I love you. Oh, I know it's quite hopeless — now that you know me for what I am, but I felt then that I had to get clean again; become a real person instead of a guilty sham. I — I don't expect you to understand, but I want to put things right again, whatever happens.' There was a short pulsing silence, then Rose's heart came to life again as she felt his hand over hers.

'I — think I understand,' he said. 'And I'm glad you told me; you've got some pluck, anyway. Now look — er — Rose, this awful business needs some thinking over, and — ' he glanced at his watch, 'I have to be back fairly soon. Could you meet me again — better make it as soon as possible — tomorrow evening?' She nodded. 'And in the meantime try not to think about it; I'll help you, if I possibly can. Eight o'clock here, then — tomorrow evening.' Rose nodded again; she could not trust herself to speak. Laurie had ignored her confession that she loved him; also he was unaware of her irrational fears of Stanton. But, thank God, she would be seeing him again on the morrow and he would tell her what she should do.

When Rose returned to the house, all was quiet. She went upstairs to her room and lay down on the bed. The weight of her misery and her dread of the unknown future swept over her and she lay there for a time drained of all energy. But presently she heard sounds from downstairs and Alison calling her. Rose roused herself and went downstairs. The little girl greeted her joyfully.

'Hello, Ray,' she said, running and putting an arm round Rose's waist. 'I thought at first you were out, as I didn't hear any sounds. Do you feel all right? You look — funny somehow.' Rose forced herself to laugh, but she put an arm round the child's shoulders and hugged her. It was a little comforting to know that Alison was fond of her; but for how long, she wondered.

For the rest of the evening Rose made a great effort to appear composed and content. She drank a sherry with Stanton before the evening meal, and was glad when he remarked that some people were coming in afterwards to play bridge. Later she joined in the game for a short time, and even managed to push her fears and apprehensions to the back of her mind. The thought of the morrow buoyed Rose with forlorn hope; for she knew in her heart that if it were humanly possible Laurie would find a way of escape from the tragic tangle she had made of her life.

The next morning and afternoon dragged interminably. Fortunately, Stanton was out most of the day, but by evening Rose was in such a state of nerves that she felt literally ill. After dinner, and hardly knowing what she was doing, Rose made some excuse about writing letters in her room, then slipped out the back way to keep her date with Laurie. She was in no state to observe the suspicious look Stanton gave her as she left the room. Not that it would have worried Rose at this stage. Soon, soon it would all be over, and she would be free of it all, not only the lies, deception, and sham, but free of Stanton's dominance. Laurie would help her.

Rose found him waiting for her in the same quiet, secluded spot. She looked at him, and sensed at once that he had surmounted the first shock at hearing her story of lies, greed and deceit. He looked down into the white, strained face with real concern, and she saw that the warmth had returned to his eyes. Suddenly he slipped a comforting arm round her shoulders. The unexpected gesture broke down Rose's self-control, and she burst into uncontrollable sobs.

'Rose,' Laurie murmured, and drew her closer to him. 'Don't, darling, please — you'll make yourself ill. Come, get in — ' and he led her hastily to the car and opened the door. 'Now listen to me. Here — take this — ' and he handed her a large handkerchief from his breast pocket. 'Now look, I have been thinking over this — problem most of the day, but before making any suggestions as to the best thing to do, I wondered what you yourself had thought of doing about it — and why. Presumably at first you had no scruples, so — ?' Rose gave a long sigh, then raised swollen eyes to his.

'Oh, but I had,' she whispered. 'I told you of the arguments I had with — Ray. It was — when it happened like that — I — it was such a temptation. Oh, how I've wished — since — ' Her voice stopped for a moment. 'I — I'd thought of going to the lawyers, but — oh, Laurie, d'you think they'll send me to prison — ? I — I actually rang the lawyers, but the secretary said I'd have to make an appointment, but I just couldn't wait a moment longer. I must get clear of it all.' Should she tell him of her dark suspicions of Stanton, Rose thought, then rejected the idea. It would all sound too fantastic, and Laurie might begin again to doubt her sanity, as she suspected that he had on first hearing her incredible story.

'You wanted to get clear of the deception and dishonesty?' Laurie asked, and as Rose murmured a fervent 'Yes, oh yes,' he drew her closer and gently kissed one pale cheek.

'Rose,' he asked very softly, 'did you mean it when you said you loved me?' She stared at him in bewilderment.

'Of course, of course,' Rose said. 'It was because of you. Laurie, I love you, and I can't bear the thought of losing you, but, don't you see, I had to risk it. I had to tell you everything, and then — lose you. You're kind and good, Laurie, but now that you know what kind of girl I am, well, I shall be eternally grateful for any help and advice you may be able to give, but — ' She could not bring herself to look at him. 'I don't expect anything else, really I don't, so — you need not think that you, that I — '

'Now, listen,' Laurie interrupted, and Rose was surprised at the ring of authority in his voice; and to think that she had once thought him diffident and shy! 'You have certainly done something which is — pretty awful, but I *can* see the temptation it must have been. I can imagine the life you'd had up to then, you poor kid, but it's good to know that you want to put things right.' He paused for a moment, then added, 'Of course, you *could* go to these lawyer people and tell them the whole story.' His voice was dubious, and Rose sat perfectly still listening to every word.

'Rose,' he looked down at the pale curve of her cheek, 'have you spent much of this money?'

'No, hardly any.' She shook her head vehemently. 'I — I think I knew in my heart that it would all have to be paid back one day; and so, what I have spent was mostly my own. You see, I had a little with me when I arrived.'

'So you *could* pay it back?' Rose nodded and waited in breathless silence. Had Laurie thought of a way of escape?

'Listen, Rose,' he said at last. 'This is my plan. We'll get married just as soon as we possibly can, then — why, what's the matter?' as she jerked upright in her seat and stared at him open-mouthed. 'You — don't you want to marry me? I thought you said — '

'Marry you!' There was a sudden break in her voice. 'Oh, Laurie, do you mean that? After all I have told you about myself; and all these lies, and the dishonesty, you still want to — marry me?' He leant forward and took both her hands in his.

'Rose, darling,' he said softly, 'I love you. I told you before, and you said you loved me, so — ' Tears started again to pour down her white cheeks.

'Oh, Laurie,' Rose said brokenly. 'Thank you, thank you. You're so good, and I — but you'll never regret it, darling — never.' There was a short, blissful silence as their lips met.

'Now listen, Ra — Rose, I mean,' Laurie whispered at last. 'We'll get married, right away, by special licence. There'll be no difficulty, and it's quick, and then we will go together to see Robert Stanton, and — and tell him all, I'm afraid. You see, darling, if we go to the solicitors — Cox and Flinders, isn't it? — well, it will then be in their hands, and — ' He paused, then hurried on. 'Whereas if we go to Stanton, and he realises that he will lose nothing at all by keeping it in the family, so to speak, he might, well, he's a decent sort of chap, and is really fond of you, Ra — Rose.'

Rose's heart was like a heavy stone in

her breast. How little Laurie knew of Stanton — or did he? Perhaps she should have told him of her fears; but it was too late now. This was the only way, and Rose knew it. And what did it matter anyway against the wonderful, unbelievable fact that Laurie still loved her, and wanted her. The heavy stone in her breast seemed to melt all at once and she felt she could face the future, whatever it held. She turned to Laurie and smiled at him.

'Yes, I'll do just as you say,' Rose said. 'How — how soon, do you think — '

'Well — ' Laurie broke in practically, 'fortunately, I'm due for leave, so it could be — could you slip up to Town the day after tomorrow, do you think?'

'Well — ' There was a worried note in Rose's voice. 'Robert won't like it, you know. I've told you how fussy he is, so — '

'I know.' Laurie looked thoughtful. 'But the reason I want to do it as soon as possible is — well, just in case he gets awkward and contacts the lawyers. Then, darling, don't you see, you will be in a much stronger position? To start with, you won't be passing under an assumed name. Not frightened of Stanton, are you?'

'No, of course not,' Rose said hastily, a little too hastily Laurie thought.

'Well, look, darling,' he said, 'hang on till you hear from me. I'll find out just how quickly it can be done, and then I'll give you a ring. Right?' Rose looked at him with all her heart in her eloquent eyes.

'I love you,' she said. 'And I'll spend the rest of my life showing you just how much.'

11

Rose started back the way she had come. It was a quiet, narrow, one-way street, which crossed the main road, and led quite soon to the back entrance of 'The Gables'. She was in a completely exalted state of mind, and though her feet moved automatically forward her head seemed to be floating in the clouds. Was it really true that quite soon she would be Laurie's wife? The fact of the confession that had to be made to Stanton came second in Rose's mind — and a poor second at that. She felt now that she could stand up to the consequences of her deception, whatever they might be. Laurie would be there to help and sustain her. Laurie would always be there. Rose sighed audibly at the thought, then, at a sudden and unusual noise behind her she glanced over her shoulder. To her amazement, she saw the headlights of a car which was turning into the narrow road. Must be someone who doesn't know the district, she thought, or he would know it is a 'one-way'. Why, there's hardly room to pass a pedestrian, let alone a car. And it's a big car, judging by the headlamps. Rose quickened her footsteps almost to a run, and took another swift glance over her shoulder. She half-expected to see the car reversing out again, but no, it was heading straight for her and gathering speed as it came. There were thick privet hedges on both sides of the road, and Rose knew that she had to get to the top of it before the car reached her. But the driver will surely see me soon, she thought breathlessly as she fairly raced along the road. Rose took another hurried glance over her shoulder; then saw to her horror that not only was the car accelerating, but it was heading straight for her. That driver must be blind or drunk, she thought in sudden panic and putting on a last frantic spurt.

Then — everything seemed to happen at once. Rose reached the junction of the roads and leapt to the left just a split second before the car was upon her. At the same moment something huge and bulky loomed up from the near side of the cross-roads. There was a screeching crash of tortured metal; Rose felt herself flung to the ground — and that was all.

Rose felt herself struggling back to consciousness, and with a great effort opened her eyes. She thought at first that it was morning and that she had just awakened from the night's sleep, for she was lying in her own bed. Then her eyes came to rest on a face that seemed to be hovering over her. It was Laurie's, and as she stared up at him the whole sequence of events of the evening rushed back into her mind. Rose flinched and gave a small cry of distress.

'Rose — ' Laurie whispered soothingly. 'It's all right, darling. You're quite safe. You got a nasty blow on the head and passed out, but you'll be all right soon. Mrs Branksome is bringing you some tea. Here she is now.' He glanced quickly towards the door as the housekeeper came forward carrying a tray. She looked tired and worried, Rose thought.

'So you are awake, Miss Ray,' she said. 'How are you feeling now?'

'Much better,' Rose murmured. 'Just a — bit of a headache. What — what happened?'

Mrs Branksome turned abruptly away after placing the tray beside Rose, and the latter was puzzled to see that her eyelids were red as if from weeping. As the housekeeper disappeared, Rose turned to Laurie who was pouring out the tea. Her eyes were shadowed with frightening memories.

'There was a smash-up, wasn't there?' she said. 'That car that was coming up behind me, and — ' She broke off for a moment and stared at him. 'Laurie, that driver must have been *quite* mad, coming along that narrow, one-way road, and at such a

speed. Oh, it's all coming back now — '
She shuddered, and Laurie spoke soothingly as he held the cup out to her.

'Drink this, Rose,' he said quietly.
'Go on, all of it, dear, and then I'll tell
you exactly what happened. Let me put
the pillows higher up behind your
shoulders. Right?' He smiled down at
her. 'Now, drink your tea like a good
girl.'

'Oh, that was good,' Rose murmured
presently. She looked up at him with a
sudden light in her eyes. 'Laurie,'
Rose's voice was hardly audible, 'are we
really — going to be married, you
— and me? I can scarcely believe it.'
She raised the cup and drank the rest of
the tea, still looking up into his face.
'Tell me — now, what happened?' He
replaced the cup, then took both her
hands in his.

'You had a very narrow escape,
darling,' he said, his hands tightening
on hers. 'The bumper just flung you
clear, but on your head, which is why
you've been out for the count for a

couple of days — and you've been under sedation. However — ' He smiled at Rose reassuringly. 'You'll be all right now.'

'My head!' Rose said weakly and put up a hand. 'So that's why it feels tight and — queer. There's a bandage?' Laurie nodded. 'But what happened to the car?' Rose asked. 'I seem to remember something — huge, coming up from the cross-roads, and then there was a terrific collision. Oh, Laurie — ?' He nodded.

'Yes, head-on.' There was a queer note in his voice, and Rose's eyes searched his face, which she now noticed was pale and drawn. 'It was a loaded lorry, and — '

'Oh,' Rose said again. 'What about the driver of the car, and the other one? Were they — ?'

'The driver of the car was killed outright, but the lorry driver escaped almost unhurt.' There was an appalled silence between them, then Rose burst out:

'I just don't understand it. The driver of that car must have been mad — quite mad. To begin with, it was a one-way street, and then to speed as he was doing, well — he must have been mad — or drunk.'

'Rose — ' Laurie interrupted quietly. 'There is something else I have to tell you. It will be a shock, I know, but — the driver of the car was *Robert Stanton*.' Rose stared at him with gathering horror, then as the full impact of his words struck her, she covered her face with her hands and shuddered. Laurie bent forward, and she felt his hand stroking her gently, soothingly.

'Rose, I can guess how you must feel about it,' he murmured. 'But, as you say, he must have been crazy to come along at such a pace, right up to the cross-roads, too. But listen, darling, I don't want you to start worrying. The inquest is tomorrow, and I am seeing to everything. He seemed to have had no relatives, but the son of an old family friend turned up and has taken Alison to stay with his mother.' Tim, Rose thought in a dazed kind of way, but she was hardly listening now to what Laurie was saying. She had dropped her hands from her face and was staring fixedly in front of her. Thoughts were scuttling to and fro in her mind like bewildered mice in a cage; and old horrifying suspicions once more came to life. Had Robert Stanton made a last attempt to be rid of her and gain the fortune which in a short time he would have known was his anyway? She would never know; there would never be an answer to her question. But, suddenly, the awfulness of the train of events which *she* had set in motion overcame her. 'Oh, God!' Rose thought. '*I* started all this. If I had not taken that first step, Robert Stanton would be alive now — and I must carry this guilt till I die; there is no escape for me. I can't marry Laurie. I'm — I'm practically a murderess — a criminal.' Rose was conscious all at once that Laurie was still speaking in a soothing murmur. She looked at him, at his fresh, boyish face — and burst into wild laughter.

'Be quiet, be quiet,' she half-sobbed. 'You don't know anything about it. Oh, leave me, leave me to myself. I must go away from here. I can't marry you now — not ever. Oh, *you* don't know — '

Then, to Rose's amazement, she felt a sharp slap on her face, and then another on the other cheek.

'Stop it, Rose,' Laurie said quite roughly, and took her firmly by the shoulders. 'Stop it — at once.' She stared at him with suddenly streaming eyes and half-smothered sobs still bursting from her throat. 'Now listen.' His voice was still sharp. 'I'm going to give you a sedative which will send you off to sleep — quite quickly, and when you wake up everything will look quite different.' His voice changed to a soothing murmur as he laid Rose gently back on the pillows, and very soon she was in a deep sleep.

When Rose awoke, it was dark and everything was quiet and still. Her mind felt clear and tranquil, and she wondered what it was that Laurie had given her to bring about such a change. But quite suddenly, black depression descended upon Rose. 'I can't marry him,' she thought despairingly, and shook her head desolately from side to side. She felt a slight movement beside her, and then came his voice.

'Awake, darling?' and a hand gently smoothed the hair from her brow. Rose looked at him, and he was puzzled and disturbed at the expression in her eyes; it was desperate but resigned. 'It's all over,' Rose was thinking. 'I'm caught again in the trap of my own making, but this time I will not drag Laurie into it with me. It's a burden I alone must bear. It's *my* punishment, and mine alone.' She tried to smile into his puzzled face, then sighed and looked away.

'Laurie, you're sweet — and kind, and I'm grateful, but — ' she looked at him with desolate eyes, 'I can't marry you, ever. I can't — no, please,' as he made a quick movement towards her. 'Don't try to persuade me; don't talk about it any more.'

'But, Rose — ' He looked completely bewildered. 'What has happened to change you so suddenly? I — just don't understand. Please, dear, tell me what is the matter.'

'No.' Her voice was flat and expressionless. 'And please don't ask, just take it as final. It — it wouldn't be fair to you.'

Laurie stared at her for a moment, then slowly the expression of his face changed.

'Rose,' he said. 'Was there — anything between you and — Stanton?'

'Oh, no, no.' Her voice was agitated all at once. 'Please don't get that idea, Laurie. We really did not get on well together at all, but — ' Rose swallowed, then added with an effort, 'Let's talk about something else.'

'But — ' He made an exasperated gesture, then stared in a baffled fashion into Rose's closed, white face. 'You really mean this, you've had second thoughts? But what will you do about — Oh, very well.' His voice was stiff, and Rose felt the tears rise to her eyes as she looked away from his bitterly hurt face. 'I'll be in tomorrow to see how you are, unless you'd — '

'Oh, no,' Rose murmured weakly. 'Please, Laurie, don't be angry.'

'Very well.' He rose abruptly to his feet, then stood for a moment looking down at her. 'Please think things over carefully, Rose, because I *want*, and I think I deserve, an explanation.' He bent suddenly and kissed her on the cheek. 'Trust me, darling,' he added in an altered tone of voice. 'Think it over, won't you?'

Rose passed a thoroughly miserable evening. 'Trust me. Think it over,' Laurie had said; and Rose did just that. She longed unspeakably to be able to confide in him, but knew that it was only a weak desire to shift yet another burden on to his shoulders. And almost her last waking thought was, 'It's no use, I've got to cope with this alone.' She took the sedative which Laurie had left with her, but just before drifting off to sleep another and rather novel thought slid into her drowsy mind. She remembered reading somewhere — and somewhen — that if one puzzled over a problem just before going off to sleep, one's subconscious mind got to work on it, and one woke — sometimes — with the solution all ready to hand. Even in the depths of her unhappiness, a wintry smile twisted Rose's mouth as she mumbled drowsily, 'Go on, subconscious, see if you can find the answer to this one.'

The sun was streaming into her room when she awoke. Mrs Branksome had just put the tray beside her, and it was the cool, pleasant tinkle of china which had awakened Rose as the housekeeper poured the tea.

'How do you feel, Miss Ray?' she asked, and Rose stared at her for a moment in wonderment. Ray, she had called her. Why, already the name was sounding strange to her ears.

'Oh, much better,' Rose said, and suddenly understood why the house-keeper looked tired and sad. 'Just ready for a cup of tea, too.' Mrs Branksome smiled with an effort and went softly out of the room. Rose drank her tea and then wondered why she herself was feeling less desperate than she had the night before. Then — she almost gasped. The subconscious! It's been working, and — Rose clasped her hands together and felt them trembling. It had come up with, well, perhaps not the solution, but something. Something which had escaped her at the time, but which this 'subconscious' had caught and held for her attention. Rose took a quick sip of her second cup of tea, then tried to marshal her thoughts. Yes, this was it! When she had asked Laurie if the driver of the car had been drunk, he had not replied. Now, Rose thought, if Robert Stanton had been out drinking it could explain why he had turned his car into a one-way street in a district which he knew very well; why he had been speeding; why he had not braked at the junction; and why he had not seen the lorry. In fact, it *could* explain everything, and it need not necessarily have anything to do with her. Rose stared unseeingly in front of her. She had no proof that Stanton had had any sinister designs upon her, ever. And she never would have now. Her former fears and suspicions could have been born and bred entirely in her own guilty imagination. As Rose looked back upon the past few months, ever since she had first come to live in Robert Stanton's house, she could see that every incident that had aroused her suspicions could be explained in a quite rational manner. And this last fatal incident which had resulted in Stanton's tragic death; well, he was a heavy drinker on occasions, and he *might* have missed the right turning. She would never know now. Rose's thoughts continued. Robert Stanton might have been perfectly genuine when he had asked her to marry him. His resentment of Laurie and his attempts to keep them from meeting could be due to quite natural jealousy, and nothing else. Even on the night of the accident Stanton might have found out that she was meeting Laurie, and he *could* have been on a drinking bout to try to forget. He *could* have — 'Oh, enough, enough,' Rose thought wearily, and passed a hand across her hot forehead, and it seemed to her then that a small voice inside her spoke to her and said, 'Rose, you will never know the truth of it. Stop thinking of yourself as a criminal; *you will never know*. But — you are young, you have your life before you. You have made a mistake — a bad mistake — but now put it all behind you. Take the happiness that fate is offering you. You may not deserve it; but how many of us do deserve the good things that come our way? Put the past behind you, and be thankful for the future — and a second chance.' Rose drew a deep breath and instinctively looked round the quiet room as if in search of the speaker. The door opened and Laurie stepped quietly in. He came to the bedside, and the two looked at each other.

'How are you, Rose?' he asked, and bent and took her hand in his. Rose felt the flood of tears behind her lids pressing to be released and tried to restrain them.

'Laurie — ' she whispered huskily, and in a moment he was down on his knees by her side.

'Darling,' he whispered, 'don't. Don't upset yourself. You didn't mean what you said last night, did you?'

'I — I don't know,' she said with difficulty. 'Laurie — ' She tried to calm herself to ask the question. 'The — the inquest. Tell me, please, was — Robert drunk at the time of the accident?' He stared at her tense face for a moment in surprise.

'Why, Ra — Rose, I mean, I did not tell you before as I knew it would upset you further; and it seemed unnecessary, anyway. But, as you have asked, well — yes, he was, *very* drunk. In fact, it was amazing that he could drive at all.'

Rose closed her eyes and clasped her hands tightly together. This surely must be the answer, she thought, and she must stop torturing herself with questions that could never now be answered.

'I'm sorry to have to tell you this, Rose, but you did ask.' She opened her eyes and looked at him. 'It's a bad business, the whole affair,' Laurie continued, rising and sitting on the side of the bed. He took both her hands and stared intently down into her face. 'You realise, don't you, that we must do a bit more thinking about — your problem?' Rose nodded, her face white and strained. Of course she had realised it.

'Yes,' she whispered almost soundlessly. 'And, I suppose, the only thing now is to go to — the lawyers?' She felt the pressure of his hands tighten over hers as he bent nearer and said in a low voice:

'Listen, Rose, I think there is another and a better way to put things right. But first, I must tell you something of Robert Stanton's affairs. According to the housekeeper, he had occasionally these bouts of heavy drinking; also he was heavily in debt and pretty well everything will have to be sold. Alison is going to be penniless.

'His experiments — well — ' Laurie shrugged. 'I think it must have become an obsession with him, and to have carried on with the tests would have cost — ' He shrugged again. 'Well, anyway, that was the position at the time of his death. Rose, did you ever suspect that he was desperate for money?' Rose nodded slowly and there was silence for a moment.

'Poor Robert,' she said at last. 'But, Laurie, it's Alison that matters now. She won't be penniless, don't you see? She is Robert's heir, the money belongs to her, but — ' She stopped suddenly and stared into his face. Laurie nodded. 'I'll have to go to the lawyers now, won't I? Oh well — '

'Just a minute, Rose,' Laurie cut in quietly. 'Let's get it quite clear.' He lowered his voice to a whisper. 'You are right, this money now belongs to Alison. That is the main point?'

Rose nodded, and felt her breath beginning to quicken. What was Laurie going to suggest?

'Well, the next point,' Laurie continued, 'is how to hand it over to the rightful owner without involving yourself in criminal proceedings. Right?' Rose nodded again, but her face had gone a little white. She took a deep breath and looked at him.

'Laurie — ' she said, 'I've given it a lot of thought, too, and — and — I am the guilty person. And — ' she gulped, 'I'm prepared to — make a clean breast of it. Perhaps when they know that I can pay every penny back, they — ' She clasped both hands tightly together and stared at him imploringly.

'Now listen, Rose,' Laurie said quietly, 'you agreed with me that the important thing is that this money belongs to Alison. Well, all we have to consider now is how to get it to her, that's all that matters really. Alison is not going to be interested in who gets punished for what, so — ' Rose stared at him.

'But, Laurie — ' she said. 'Don't you understand, I deserve to be punished for what I did. I — '

'Well, how many of us *do* get our deserts?' His tone was practical. 'Rose, you've let this thing get all out of proportion. I am certainly not minimising what you did, but you have been honest about it, and are willing to make full amends. Now — if you can make full amends, without punishing yourself publicly, then why not do it? You have repented, confessed, and are willing to take your punishment. Surely that's fair enough; unless, of course, you want to be a martyr.'

'Oh, Laurie, of course I don't, but,

can't you see, it isn't right that I should go — unpunished?'

'You won't,' he said quietly. 'Make no mistake about that. This is something you will never be able to forget — ever, and that in itself will be a long drawn-out punishment. Now — ' He smiled and patted her cheek. 'Don't you want to know what my suggestion is?' Rose nodded, not trusting herself to speak.

'Well — ' He grinned down at her. 'Come on, cheer up: this is a super plan. *One*. We'll get married just as soon as you are on your feet. *Two*. We'll adopt Alison as our daughter. *Three*. We'll open a bank account for her, or a trust fund, or put the money into building shares in her name — the lot. It may stay there till she is of age, and then — well, it'll be up to her. Now, what do you think of that for an idea?'

Rose was staring at him with her mouth half-open, and she could feel her breath coming rapidly and unevenly.

She had never thought of any plan remotely like this, but — was this the answer? Was the self-made trap to open at last and set her free? She stared at Laurie and had an insane desire to burst out laughing. This plan put forward by Laurie seemed fantastic — and yet wonderful, too. To have living with her the two people she loved most in the world — indeed, the only two. But — Rose's second reaction was that it could not be done. It was too — simple; and yet, why not? The money belonged to Alison, and Laurie's plan meant that it could be kept safe for her till she was of age. Also she would have a home, and a loving home if Rose had anything to do with it. Ah, but what of those lawyers whose job it was to administer the estate? Would they not consider it strange that she wanted to make over such a large sum of money to a child who was no relation? Well — Rose looked again at Laurie and saw that he was waiting eagerly for her to speak.

'Well, what do you think?' he asked impatiently.

'I — well, it — it sounds marvellous,' Rose jerked out. 'But — Laurie, wouldn't the lawyers think, well, think it a bit — queer? I mean for me to 'give' away all that money to a child who is not even a relative?' He thought for a moment, a frown between his eyes.

'Well — I don't know,' he said at last. 'Let's put it this way. You will be my wife, yes?' Rose's eyes glowed and a blush stained her cheek as he bent forward and kissed her. 'So — you will be my responsibility, yes?' She smiled and nodded. 'Right. You haven't any use for all that money.' Rose looked dubious and slightly puzzled; but Laurie continued: 'You've probably never given this a thought, darling, but as a matter of fact, though I'm a man of simple tastes, I'm also quite well off. Now, Alison, so far as the lawyers know, is left penniless, with not a relative in the world. Why, then, should it seem strange that you, with a well-endowed husband, should want to make provision for a child whom you love and whom we have adopted as a daughter? In any case, darling, you need not transfer the whole lot, all at once. Do it by degrees. Anyway, what does it matter what those stuffy old solicitors think? They will have to obey your instructions.'

'Oh, darling,' Rose almost wailed. 'It's a wonderful plan, but, don't you see, those lawyers — Mr Cox is such a nice man, too — they will think I am someone to be *admired*, instead of, oh — '

Laurie looked at her, then burst out laughing. 'Rose, you obstinate little idiot, why are you so determined to be a criminal?' he asked. 'This plan is a good one, and it achieves its object; and that's all that matters.' He looked at her soberly for a moment, then added, 'Don't you see that you are being selfish if you reject a plan that safeguards the rights of Alison, the only person who matters in this connection; and insisting on something that will bring misery and unhappiness not only to yourself, but also to me, *and* Alison whom you say you love, and the various friends and acquaintances we both have. And all for nothing, or rather, just to satisfy your craving to rid yourself of the feeling of guilt. I suppose it doesn't matter about other people's feelings so long as you feel right again with yourself and the world?' Rose stared at Laurie with lips gone suddenly dry. Never had he spoken to her like this before; she could hardly believe that it was he who had spoken so coldly and angrily. But was he right? *Was* she being selfish? In her almost feverish desire to clear herself of the atmosphere of deceit and lies which had hung over her for so long, was she also sacrificing the happiness of those she loved? She turned her head from side to side as Laurie began to speak again.

'Rose,' he said quite unemotionally, 'you asked my advice. Well, I've given it to you, and I honestly believe that my plan meets all the needs. Why *invite* punishment for something you have done wrong? Be thankful that it is not necessary. Look at it this way, Rose: may it not be that a merciful providence, or Father if you like, has come forward with the answer?' There was a silence as Rose became very still. She stared at him for a moment, then, with a half-sob, half-laugh, she raised herself and flung both arms round his neck.

'Oh, what a blind fool I am.' Her voice was unsteady. 'Darling, you're right, of course you are right. Why did I ever doubt it? It *is* a wonderful plan. Of course you know best, darling. Why — ' She raised her face and looked into his eyes. 'You couldn't give me advice that wasn't *good*.'

12

Rose spent the next couple of weeks in a maze of conflicting emotions. Sometimes she wondered if she were not moving in a dream; a wonderful, enthralling yet bewildering dream. She and Laurie had slipped quietly up to London and been married by special licence. Rose remembered the moment of terror she had had when she suddenly remembered her false passport. But Laurie seemed to know all the answers, and promptly allayed her fears.

'We need not worry about that yet,' he told her. 'Later on, when we get round to having a honeymoon, you will be included on mine, as my wife. We need not mention the other one. Your true particulars will be at Somerset House, I suppose.' He looked at her questioningly, and Rose hesitated.

'I don't really know,' she said at last.

'I was born in India, and registered out there.' She looked a bit worried as she went on. 'I have heard, though, from other people, that since the Partition, papers were lost and it was terribly difficult to establish — '

'Well, that's just the job,' Laurie said, laughing. 'We need not worry about that, then.' Rose looked at him in amazement. She had thought him shy and diffident, but during the last few weeks he had shown qualities of initiative and leadership that she would not have expected. Yet, with it all, he was still modest and simple in outlook. 'He has an inner strength,' Rose thought, 'and I am lucky to have him for a husband. Why, he is everything a girl could possibly want.'

Laurie and Rose were living for the time being at a small, old-fashioned hotel fairly near the hospital. Only Laurie's closest friends knew of the marriage, and in view of Robert Stanton's sudden and tragic death, the reason seemed obvious. 'The Gables' and all its contents was up for sale. But now there was Alison to think of. The child had written to ask when she could come home, and though they knew that she was being well looked after, Rose felt that she was fretting. They had decided to tell the child of their plans for her future when she returned. Rose had a secret worry of her own. In the midst of her happiness a question kept recurring in her mind. Farndon, and Laurie's job here. Did he want to stay? Would he mind very much if Rose suggested a change? She was reluctant to raise the subject; he had been so good to her, so unselfish, and Rose herself loved him so much that she would have been perfectly happy to share a desert island with him. And that was the point. A desert island or anywhere would be preferable to Farndon with its associations of lies, deceit and terror. Rose longed unspeakably to get away from it all; longed to get right away to a place, any place, where she could really start again, and put all the misery and shame behind her for ever. Once or twice her thoughts turned to India with an aching nostalgia. But she knew that that was not the answer. Her past would be certain to catch up with her. But in spite of all this, Rose knew that if Laurie wished to stay she would not utter a word to dissuade him, and she would never let him know how she felt.

This afternoon the two of them were sitting in the quiet little lounge of the hotel having tea. Rose looked at her young husband, and all her love for him was in her brilliant dark eyes. He smiled across at her.

'Happy, darling?' he asked, and for reply she moved slightly and leaned her head against his shoulder.

'I didn't know that anyone could be so gloriously happy,' she murmured, then looked quickly round and raised her head as a sound came from the door. It was the clerk from the reception desk and he was looking towards them. Rose made a face at Laurie.

'I expect it's a telephone call for you,' she said. 'Doctors don't seem to have much peace.' Laurie glanced at the man, but he was looking straight at Rose.

'It's for you, Mrs Drake,' he said. 'There's a gentleman asking for you — for Miss Ray Desmond, he said — name of Trent.'

'For me!' Rose stared at Laurie, then nodded her thanks to the man, who left the room at once. Her heart was beginning to beat with frightening uneven thuds, for the name Trent had a vaguely familiar ring. Who was this man Trent? Did she know him? And what did he want of her? Perhaps it was someone from Cox and Flinders. Perhaps —

'Something to do with Alison, I expect,' Laurie said, then suddenly stared into her worried face. 'What's the matter, love? Look, I'd better come with you.' He rose quickly to his feet, drawing her with him. 'Come along, we'll beard this lion together. D'you know the name? Does it ring a bell?' There was a vaguely distressed look on Rose's face.

'I've got a feeling that I should know it,' she said slowly as they walked together to the door; and could have added that the feeling was also ominous.

'Someone you knew in India, perhaps,' Laurie suggested. 'Well, anyway, there he is; must be, as he's the only chap here.' Rose followed the direction of his eyes — and her heart slowly froze. Oh, yes, she knew this man, though for the moment she had forgotten the name. He was the man who had paid her attentions on the ship before Ray's death; and then, later, had tried to start an affair with her. She remembered how she had snubbed him contemptuously, and then had regretted the possibility of making an enemy of him.

'Know him?' Laurie asked in a low

tone as the man half-turned and stared at Rose. He thought he detected a look of slight dismay in the stranger's slightly bloodshot eyes. Looks as if he has been drinking, Laurie thought, and looked sideways at Rose. She nodded. Though her chin was held high and she faced the man squarely, there was terror and despair in her heart. What did this man know? What was he going to say?

'Good afternoon, Mr Trent,' Rose said, and by some miracle managed to keep her voice level and cool. 'You wanted to see me?' The man nodded, then glanced swiftly at Laurie.

'I'd like to see you alone,' he said to Rose.

'My wife's business is also mine,' Laurie said quietly. 'You'd better come into the lounge, I think; there is no one there.' The man stared, then seemed to hesitate.

'So — ' he said, looking at Rose, 'you are married. The chap at the desk said he thought it was your maiden name.' Then, with an air of bravado, he turned to Laurie. 'O.K., if that's the way you want it.' He laughed. 'But you won't like it, y'know.' With a swagger he followed Rose and Laurie into the still empty lounge.

'Well now, what is it?' Laurie asked, turning to confront Trent, and retaining his hold of Rose's arm.

'It's her I wanted to see,' the man said truculently. 'She's a phoney, d'you hear? She's no more Miss Ray Desmond that I am. At least — ' his lip curled in an ugly manner, 'I suppose you are married. What did she call herself before, eh?'

'Look here — ' Laurie began angrily, but Rose suddenly gripped him by the arm.

'You must be mad — or drunk,' she said, forcing her voice to sound scornful. 'How dare you suggest that we are not married. This gentleman who is my husband is Mr Laurie Drake, a doctor at Farndon hospital. Now, what evidence have you for making such a charge?'

A shade of doubt crossed Trent's swarthy face, but at once he thrust his hand into an inner pocket and pulled out a wallet.

'You can't get away from this,' he said, and from the wallet he drew out a roll of what looked like receipted bills. Rose at once recognised them as 'chits' issued by the ship's bars for drinks, cigarettes, etc. They were all clipped together, but Trent carefully extracted one, and held it out for them both to see. 'That your signature?' he asked, and stared into Rose's face. She glanced at it briefly, and her heart gave a jolt of fear as the whole scene came back to her. Ray and she sitting on the deck with Trent between them. She remembered clearly signing the chit for two drinks for herself and Ray before he had joined them and ordered more. But how had this particular chit come into his possession, for Rose could see her own sprawling signature at the foot of the page.

'Well, it looks like it,' she admitted,

trying to keep the tremor of fear from her voice. 'But what of it; and how did it come into your possession?' He laughed coarsely.

'Let's say the steward made a mistake and put it in with mine. The point is — if that's your signature, then you're not, or shall we say, were not, Ray Desmond.' He leered at her triumphantly. 'I knew it was the other girl, I heard you call her Ray. We were sitting on the deck, remember? But of course you won't.'

Rose laughed. Her early tough training in the paddling of her own canoe was coming to her aid.

'But I do,' she said, then, after a pause, 'So what?' Trent glared at her for a moment, then continued, looking slightly dashed.

'I've been trying for a long time to trace you,' he said. 'The other girl, the one who looked like you, but hadn't got your — ' He grinned, then stepped quickly back as Laurie made a threatening move towards him. 'Well, anyway,

276

the one who — very conveniently died, she was the one with the lolly, not you. And that's why you did it; to get the money. I was never sure that you were the right one. Then, when I came across that chit among my papers, well — '

Rose's heart was pounding against her ribs, but she laughed again, and was about to reply when Laurie cut in. He had been listening quietly, but now thought it time to intervene.

'Look here, you must be mad,' he said to Trent, 'and most offensive. This lady is my wife, and the only money she has is what she shares with me. As for the name, I mean my wife's maiden name,' he laughed contemptuously, 'let me have a look at this — document.' He waited while Trent hesitated, then held out the chit for Laurie to see. The latter gave it a cursory glance, burst out laughing and turned to Rose.

'Darling, this awful squiggle *is* your signature, I suppose?' he said. 'Well, I guess I should be used to it by now. But — ' he stared coolly into the other man's glowering face, 'it could be anything, couldn't it? What was the other girl's name, anyway? Look — ' He turned to Rose for a moment, then looked back into Trent's sullen face. 'I've a good mind to have you thrown out. Suppose this is my wife's signature, almost illegible though it is, what about it? You haven't yet told us what the other girl was called.'

'Well, there it is,' Trent said belligerently, and pointing to the chit. 'Read it for yourself.'

'You read it,' Laurie suggested. 'I must confess I can't.'

'It's R. Delmont. I checked up at the shipping office.' Trent's voice was triumphant. Laurie took another look at the paper and laughed.

'Well, it doesn't really matter,' he said. 'The point is, what proof have you of this cock-and-bull story? Any witnesses who saw which of these two girls signed this paper? And the other point: any witness who heard my wife call the other girl Ray? Well?'

Trent stared at him, then at Rose, then burst out violently:

'It's true, I tell you. I saw her sign the chit, and I heard her. I — '

'Where's your proof?' Laurie cut in swiftly, then as the man made no reply, 'Of course, you haven't any. Such a damn-fool story. What's your game, eh?' He took a threatening step forward. 'Now, clear out before I have you thrown out.' Rose looked at Trent. His coarse face was suffused with blood, and his thick lips were compressed.

'All right, Mr High-and-Mighty,' he almost spat at them, 'I'll go,' and turned to the door. 'But you haven't heard the end of this. I'll be back tomorrow — after I've made a few more enquiries.'

'Get out,' Laurie said, and with one last furious glance he went.

As the door closed behind him, Rose sank nervelessly on to the settee. 'Oh, Laurie — ' she began, twisting her hands together, but with a swift gesture he silenced her; then with noiseless strides crossed over to the door and threw it open. Rose watched as he looked both ways along the passage, and then returned.

'It's all right,' Laurie said in a low tone. 'He's gone, the slimy — '

'But, Laurie, it was true, what he said.' Rose's voice was low-pitched and full of foreboding. 'Oh, darling, what do you think he'll do?' He sat down beside her and passed an arm round her shoulders.

'Do?' he said, drawing her close to him. 'Just nothing, of course. Darling, pull yourself together; you stood up well to him. Now — ' He looked into her worried face. 'What *could* he do? Darling, think carefully. *Did* anyone see you sign that chit? And was anyone near when you addressed the other girl as Ray? Now, cast your mind back and *think*.' Rose drew a deep breath and there was silence for a moment in the quiet room.

'No,' she said at last quietly but with

conviction. 'Apart from the steward who took the chit, there was no one else anywhere near. In fact, I remember remarking to Ray about how empty the deck was. You see, it was late afternoon, and I suppose most people were dressing for dinner. Yes, darling, I'm quite sure of that.' He gave her shoulders a quick squeeze and dropped a kiss on her cheek.

'Then, in my opinion, you have nothing to worry about,' he said. 'We can count out the Goanese steward. With the hundreds of chits that would pass through his hands, and even supposing Trent could 'get' at him, what would his word be worth? And as for the name — ' He laughed and gave Rose another squeeze. 'Honestly, it *could* be anything. But, of course, the thing is, darling, he hasn't a shred of proof of anything, so — there's no case. Now, put it right out of your head, love. Let's have a drink, shall we?' But Rose continued to look worried.

'He said we hadn't heard the end of

it,' she reminded Laurie. 'And he threatened to come tomorrow. D'you think — ?'

'He'll not come tomorrow, or the day after, or the day after that,' he said confidently. 'You'll see. Why, the chap hadn't a leg to stand on — and he knew it. Didn't you notice the furious, frustrated look on his face?'

'Well, of course,' Rose admitted. 'But still — '

'We'll just wait and see,' Laurie said. 'We've only to wait till tomorrow, and I shall be very surprised indeed if we ever hear again from Mr Trent.'

Rose worried off and on for the rest of the evening, and for most of the next day, and as the evening approached she found it almost impossible to fix her thoughts on anything but the threatening Mr Trent. She refused to go out and Laurie did not press her, knowing what her state of mind must be. He knew that from minute to minute her ears were listening for a call from the reception desk. But the whole afternoon and evening passed without a sign from Trent.

'What did I tell you?' Laurie asked. 'You'll not hear another word from that would-be blackmailer.' Rose gave him her brilliant smile, almost the first since the previous afternoon. She sighed deeply and straightened her shoulders as if freeing herself from a heavy load.

'Yes, it does rather look like it,' she agreed; and even as she spoke they both heard the sharp ring of the telephone in the hall. The two looked at each other silently, and waited. Then they heard a man's footsteps nearing the door of the lounge. It was the clerk from the reception desk, and as before he looked across at Rose.

'For you, Mrs Drake,' he called from the door. 'A gentleman asking for you. The line's a bit faint, but the name sounded like Tennant.'

'Thank you,' Rose said in a carefully-controlled voice. 'I'll — come right away.' As the man vanished, she rose to her feet, but Laurie was before her.

'Shall I take it?' he asked, anxiously

watching her face, which had gone quite white.

'No,' Rose said, 'I'll go.'

'Then I'll come with you,' Laurie said, and took her arm.

'I put the call through to the writing-room, Madam,' the clerk said and motioned to the open door. Hardly knowing what she did, Rose went in, followed by Laurie, and lifted the receiver. Laurie put an arm round her waist, and watched her face intently as she started to speak. He could see the effort she was making to remain calm.

'Hello, Mrs Drake speaking,' Rose said in a faintly breathless voice. 'Who — ' She waited for a moment. 'Who — did you say?' There was another short silence, then Rose spoke again. 'I'm sorry, I can't hear very well, the line — yes, yes, that's better. Yes, of course that will be all right. Yes — we'll let you know, and — thank you very much, it's very kind of you. Goodbye.'

With trembling hand Rose replaced the receiver, and almost collapsed against Laurie's shoulder. Her breath came in a great sigh.

'Well — ' she said faintly, and he laughed and squeezed her round the waist.

'Well — ' he mimicked. 'I presume that the call was not from our Mr Trent.'

'No,' she said, and broke into almost hysterical laughter. 'Oh, Laurie, what a relief. I feel quite sick. No, it was young Tim Tennant; you know, Alison is staying with his mother. And it was just to say that they had got my letter, and would be delighted to keep Alison till our affairs are settled and we can have her with us. Oh, Laurie, isn't that marvellous? Kiss me, darling, I feel wonderful.'

Laurie needed no second invitation, and then the two went back to the lounge.

'Let's have a drink,' Laurie suggested, then asked, 'Oh, by the way, what did you say his name was? Tennant — umm — it is rather like — '

'Shh — ' Rose said, 'I never want to hear that name again.' She smiled at him, and there was another short blissful silence as he bent his face to hers.

'I don't think I want a drink, darling,' Rose said softly. 'Let's go to bed, shall we?'

As the two walked up the stairs to their room, Laurie glanced fondly at Rose's lovely face and said:

'Feeling happier now, darling?' She nodded, and smiled, then said:

'If there is nothing tomorrow, and the day after, and the day after that, well, I'll just put all thoughts of that beastly man right out of my mind — for always.'

13

And the next day passed without a sign from Trent; and the day after that. Indeed, the whole week; and Rose really began to breathe again. Laurie was right, she thought thankfully. What a lucky girl I am. Another week went by, and one morning at the beginning of the third week Rose had a letter from Alison.

'Darling Ray' (it began), and Rose paused for a moment to wonder how she was going to explain the change of name to the child, then continued reading. 'When can I come to live with you and Laurie? Auntie Maud (Tim's mother) told me that you had married each other. I was very glad. I am longing to see you again. Have you got a house yet? Cozen Tim said I must stay here till you have got a house. Of course I am quite happy here, but I do miss you. Lugs sends his love, and so do I. Please rite soon. Yours loving Alison. xxxxxxx'

When Laurie came in at lunch-time Rose showed him the letter.

'You can see the kid's terribly homesick,' she said, and looked at him uncertainly. 'D'you think the adoption business will take long? I do wish we could have her with us, Laurie.' Rose was wondering again about Laurie's job here, and whether it would be fair to broach the subject of a move. It did seem to her that for all their sakes, Alison's included, a complete break with Farndon would be a good thing. But still she hesitated, then went off at a slight tangent.

'Darling,' she said, with a grin, 'how am I going to explain my change of name?'

'Easy,' Laurie said airily. 'I shall tell her that I always thought the name Rose was just made for you. I bet you anything she will agree; children love flower names, and in no time at all the old name will be forgotten.'

'But what about other people?' Rose demurred. 'Not that I have made many friends here — I wasn't allowed to. And I was still on formal terms with them all, but still — ' She looked at him and took a deep breath. Now's the time, she thought. 'What I mean is, if we are staying in Farndon, there may be some awkward — '

'Yes, I thought about that some time ago,' Laurie interrupted, laying Alison's letter down on the table, 'and I thought the very best thing for everyone would be to get right away — and give you a chance to start all over again. Somewhere where you can really put the past behind you, among people you have never met before. In fact, a clean slate, darling. Hey, hey, what's the matter?' for Rose had rushed and put both arms round his neck and was hugging him to her.

'Oh, darling, darling Laurie,' she said, and stopped for a brief moment to kiss him. 'That's what I want more than anything else in the world. Where — where did you think of going, and when? Oh, gosh! This is marvellous.' She stopped again to hug and kiss him anew, and Laurie returned the caresses with interest.

'Well — ' he said, watching Rose's face, 'I had thought of Tasmania — ' and Rose gave another shriek of excitement. 'I've heard it's a lovely little country with a delightful climate.'

'Darling — ' Rose breathed. Her cheeks were bright pink, and her big eyes shone like stars. 'It sounds — ' she caught her breath, then finished on a long sigh, 'just heavenly. Let's write about it straightaway. Oh, Laurie, I can hardly wait.' He grinned at her teasingly.

'I've already written,' he said, then dodged neatly as she aimed a blow at him.

'Oh, I could kick you,' Rose said in mock anger. 'Why didn't you tell me before? I suppose you'll be saying next that you've already got a job in

Tasmania, *and* that we go tomorrow, eh?' He laughed.

'Now, don't be impatient, darling; it's not till next week, as a matter of fact.' Rose gave another squeal of excitement. She stared at him in amazement.

'Next week,' she exclaimed, 'but — well, *have* you got a job, then?'

'Of course,' Laurie said, then burst out laughing. 'Darling, if you could see your face! Yes, I've got a job in Hobart.' He paused, watching her, then said softly, 'Pleased, darling, really?'

'Oh!' Rose pressed her cheek to his, and he could feel the tears. 'I just don't deserve all my blessings,' she said huskily. 'Dear Laurie. Providence, or — God, perhaps, must be very forgiving, *and* I am so grateful, so grateful. She was silent for a moment, then raised her head to look at him with the tears still bright in her eyes. 'Will it be all right about Alison?' she asked.

'Yes, love,' Laurie replied. 'No difficulty there. If the adoption papers are not through by the time we have to leave, she can come with us for a holiday. She won't be left behind, darling, not on any account.' In the blissful silence that followed there came the sound of a knock at the door. It was a quiet, almost furtive knock, and Laurie and Rose looked towards the door and then at each other. The bright, excited colour slowly faded from Rose's cheeks. The Trent episode had not quite faded from her mind. The knock came again.

'Who can that be, Laurie?' Rose whispered half-fearfully, but he called out a cheerful:

'Come in, whoever you are.' There was a pause, then the door was pushed slowly open and a face appeared in the aperture.

'Alison!' they both said at once, and Rose got quickly to her feet.

'Alison, where on earth have you come from?' she asked.

'Oh, Ray!' and the child streaked across the room and flung herself into Rose's outstretched arms. 'I just couldn't stay away any longer. Please, you don't mind, do you? You're not cross with me? I left a note for Auntie Maude — Oh, Ray, it's so lovely to see you again. Can I stay now, with you and Laurie — for always?' Rose laughed with the tears in her eyes as she hugged the child to her.

'Of course you can stay,' she said. 'Can't she, Laurie?' She looked at Laurie, and he grinned and nodded. 'In fact, listen, Alison, here's some news which I know will make you feel fine.' The little girl stared at her wonderingly.

'What is it?' she asked in a tense little voice, a voice which made Rose realise the strain the child had been undergoing.

'You are going to stay with Laurie and me for always.'

Other titles in the
Linford Romance Library:

SEASONS OF CHANGE

Margaret McDonagh

When Kathleen Fitzgerald left Ireland twenty years ago, she never planned to return. In England she married firefighter Daniel Jackson and settled down to raise their family. However, when Dan is injured in the line of duty, events have a ripple effect, bringing challenges and new directions to the lives of Dan, Kathleen and their children, as well as Kathleen's parents and her brother, Stephen. How will the members of this extended family cope with their season of change?

CHERRY BLOSSOM LOVE

Maysie Greig

Beth was in love with her boss, but he could only dream of the brief passionate interlude he had shared with a Japanese girl long ago, and of the child he had never seen. Beth agrees to accompany him to Japan in search of his daughter. There perhaps, the ghost of Madame Butterfly would be laid, and he would turn to her for solace . . . Her loyal heart is lead along dark and dangerous paths before finding the love she craves.

THE SEABRIGHT SHADOWS

Valerie Holmes

Elizabeth, bound to a marriage she wants no part in, is strong willed and determined to free herself from the arrangement her father Silas has made. But she is trapped. The family's fortunes are linked to and dependent upon her marriage to Mr Timothy Granger, a man she despises. It takes a bold act of courage and the interference of her Aunt Jessica to make her see the future in a different light and save the family from ruin.

THE TWO OF US

Jennifer Ames

When Mark Dexter, visiting Australia, invited Janet to work in his publishing house in the United States, she thought he was offering her heaven. They had an adventurous and thrilling trip by plane to New York, lingering in Fiji and Havana; but when they reached New York Janet found she could not get away from Julian Gaden, an odd character whom Mark had introduced her to in a Sydney night club . . .